Night

of the

Carpathia

Look for these other exciting
Autumn Harbor Press books
from Joe Tompkins!

The Sleeping Beauty
Overslept Series

Book 1 - Sleeping Beauty Overslept

Book 2 - Sidhera's Revenge

Book 3 - The Travelling Coins

Night

of the

Carpathia

Joe Tompkins

Autumn Harbor Press

Atlanta, GA

Night

of the

Carpathia

© 2013 by Joe Tompkins
All Rights Reserved

Autumn Harbor Press

FIRST EDITION

September 2013

ISBN 978-0-9825732-4-2

For more information about Autumn Harbor books, please visit our website @ www.autumnharbor.com

This book is for my sister, Carrie, whose sincere enthusiasm about everything (including the Titanic) has always been a blessing in my life.

There have been critical moments throughout history in which, often unknown to those involved, the choices of a single person have forever changed the world and everything that follows.

- Minerva Dumas
Founder, *HistCorp*

Only the fool, fixed in his folly, may think
He can turn the wheel on which he turns.

- T. S. Eliot

Chapter One

On April 11, 1912, with the evening sun a radiant ember peeking through the stone and glass crevasses of the New York City skyline behind her, the steamship Carpathia made her way through the harbor towards gathering storm clouds over the open sea ahead.

She was a beautiful ship, with a long steel bow topped by four towering masts that were laden with cranes and rigging instead of sails. A modest-sized passenger liner by the standards of the day, she nevertheless cut an impressive figure sliding between the clusters of smaller sailing ships in the harbor. A single red funnel rose up from her center, ringed with a strip of black at the top. A light wisp of smoke drizzled from her chimney as she wove through the harbor traffic, but once out at sea, the firemen stoking the boilers below would pour on the coal and she would run up to cruising speed, leaving a long cloud of black smoke trailing behind her across the open Atlantic.

Passengers had lined up along the railings on all decks, blankets pulled around them in the chilly wind. They watched as twilight fell over the sprawling city that curled around the bay. Some were laughing or talking as they huddled together. Some waved back at the city as if to say goodbye. From somewhere on the ship, the sounds of a band playing drifted up through the pipes and vents and mingled with the evening wind.

On the bare mast closest to the front of the ship, in a small, bucket-shaped platform that served as the ship's forward lookout station, Olivia Grace watched the clouds above the city set ablaze by the fading sun. Although the wind whipped her long, curly tangle of reddish-brown hair around her, she was able to keep out of the worst of it by crouching low in the shelter of the crow's nest. This high up, she could feel the giant steamship rocking gently from side to side as it made its way through the harbor, but the motion didn't bother Olivia in the least. She barely noticed it as she peered out at the receding skyline as she had so many times before.

Olivia's father was one of the firemen who stoked the fires and kept the massive boilers running below. She knew that he would be going on shift soon. When they cleared the harbor, Captain Rostron would order the ship up to cruising speed and her father would be working tirelessly for the next twelve hours until he collapsed at the end of his shift. She wanted to go down and see him before then... to kiss his cheek before it became a mask of oily soot. She could stay a little longer, though. Just a few more minutes...

Olivia watched the sprawling skyline and imagined the little brown brick house off of 5th that they had once called home... the one with the chipped front step that her mother would tease her father about getting fixed someday. She strained her eyes, imagining that she could see that little house as it faded into the gathering twilight.

There was a stir in the crowd below. People cheering and clapping.

2

Olivia turned to see the Statue of Liberty passing on starboard. The captain had brought them in close to give the passengers a good view. From her crouched position high up in the crow's nest, the statue seemed to loom directly above Olivia. Lady Liberty's masklike expression was partially shrouded in the gathering shadows. Her blank and weathered gaze sent a shiver through Olivia as they cruised slowly past it. The headwind picked up and gusted through the rigging around her, letting out a mournful wail and drowning out the excited murmurs of the huddled families below.

Olivia had lingered longer than she should have in her hidden perch, and now she was worried that she might not catch her father before his shift began. She climbed down the long ladder with practiced speed, and her feet had just touched the deck when a voice from behind her made her jump.

"You shouldn't be up there little girl!" the voice said sternly.

Olivia wasn't fooled, though. She turned around with her hands on her hips. "Bubs, I've told you not to sneak up on me like that and I've told you that I can go anywhere I good and well please. I'm twelve years old and practically a grown woman."

Standing before her was a mouse-like boy of ten, dressed in a tattered burlap shirt that was two sizes too big for him. The sleeves, although he tried to keep them rolled up, were forever hanging down over his hands, making him look even smaller than he already was.

"Didn't I fool you even a little bit? For just a second you thought I was an officer that caught you sneaking down from the crow's nest, didn't you?"

Olivia scoffed. "Your voice sounds more like a little girl's than a grown man. Now if you'll excuse me, I need to get down to the engine room before the captain calls for engines ahead."

Bubs seemed unaffected by Olivia's haughty attitude, being quite used to her often inexplicable and abrupt mood changes. He fell into step beside her as she made her way towards the aft stairwell. "Hey, I think there may be a jewel thief onboard." he said, grinning excitedly.

Olivia snorted. "There is not."

"I saw 'em!" Bubs nodded earnestly. "I passed him in the second class corridor on the way to his cabin. He was carrying around this big brown suitcase and Jimmy the porter came up and offered to help carry it to the man's room. Boy-oh-boy you shoulda seen the look this guy gave Jimmy. 'No one touches this case but me!' he yelled, and hurried off with the case hugged up all close to his chest."

"That is odd behavior." Olivia admitted. "It does not, however, mean that the man is a jewel thief."

Bubs shook his head adamantly. "Well he sure didn't want Jimmy's hands on that suitcase of his. What do *you* think he's got in it that's made him so jumpy?"

Olivia shrugged. "It could have been a million things. Maybe it was his collection of porcelain kitty cats and he didn't want Jimmy hauling it around like a brute and breaking something."

Bubs looked appalled. "Porcelain kitty cats? Why would a guy be carrying around something crazy like that? No. It was most *definitely* stolen jewels. Probably diamonds."

"If you say so." Olivia sighed, rolling her eyes to herself. Bubs was just two years younger than her, but sometimes he had the most childish ideas. She ducked into the narrow stairwell that led to the engine room and was thankful when Bubs didn't follow.

Once below decks, the ship became a maze of corridors and dead-ends that confounded most passengers, but was comfortably familiar to Olivia. Here in the second-class area, the air still held the lingering aroma of fresh paint from the most recent touch-up, and the carpet that lined the hallways was immaculate and spotless. She passed some passengers just coming in from the decks, pulling off their blankets and trying to clap some warmth into their chapped hands. Despite it being April, passengers were often surprised at how cold the air was once they were away from land. Because they were heading for the balmy Mediterranean, most first-timers never thought to bring warm clothes for the week-long Atlantic crossing.

Olivia ducked past the shivering passengers and into an inconspicuous door with the words "Crew Only" stenciled across it.

Once she stepped into the crew section of the ship, everything became whitewashed iron and steel. No carpets or wood paneling here. Olivia descended down the metal steps and could now hear the rumbling of the massive engines, feeling the powerful thrum in the walls and beneath her feet.

After several more flights of stairs and winding corridors, Olivia reached a massive bulkhead door that said "Engine Room- No Admittance". She had to lean into it with all of her weight to make it move, and when she could finally step through, a blast of heat pressed over her, making her cringe.

The sound here was almost deafening, and the pounding of the giant ship's engines that had felt like only a tremor on the decks above now shook the floor under her feet so hard that it made her teeth clatter. The acrid smell of burning coal and smoke assaulted her at once and made her eyes begin to water. Even though the engines had not yet been stoked up to full cruising speed, the heat in the cavernous room was unbearable, drenching Olivia in sweat before she had taken three steps inside.

Olivia ran to a ladder in a nearby alcove and flew down the rungs. She descended into a small, dark room lined with tables and wooden benches. Metal ashtrays held dozens of still-smoking cigarette remains and a choking cloud of tobacco smoke hung low in the air.

When Olivia saw that the room was empty, her heart sank. *She was too late! He had already gone on shift!*

She ran to the heavy door on the opposite side of the room and yanked it open. There she saw a dozen men walking into the chaotic din of the firing room, pulling on gloves and masks. They were already a good distance down the corridor, but near the back of the group, walking with his unmistakable limp, she recognized her father.

"Daddy!" she yelled into the deafening turmoil, and she jumped forward to catch up with him. Before she could move, though, she was yanked back roughly by her collar.

"No bilge rats allowed down here! You been told that!"

Olivia pulled herself free and spun to find the foreman, Curly Reynolds, glaring down at her. With a massive bald head and a sour, brutish face, Curly was just about the meanest-looking man Olivia had ever seen. His bushy tangle of a mustache still held the crusty pieces of his last meal clinging to the whiskers and his sneering upper lip unveiled a crooked mess of yellowed teeth underneath. Atop his meaty head was a lump above his right ear that looked like someone had recently hit him up aside his skull with a hammer. The lump had been there since the first time she had ever seen him, though… and that was almost a year ago.

Olivia looked again over her shoulder at her father as he walked away towards his shift. She felt the desperate urge to run after him anyway, but she wouldn't put it past Curly to cuff her on the side of the head if she tried.

She spun back towards the foreman. "I just wanted to see him before he went on shift!" she shouted angrily over the noise.

Curly snorted. "You'll live. My kids haven't seen me in eighteen months. You can bet they're not crying about it."

You're probably right about that. Olivia thought furiously. *I don't see how anyone would ever miss a troll like you.*

6

"You might get special treatment from Captain Rostron," Curly continued, "but down here what I say goes, and any little bilge rats skulking around my boilers will get squashed under my boot."

Olivia swallowed and couldn't help but cut a quick, nervous glance down at Curly's massive, heavy boots, which were caked with filth.

"Olivia?" came a voice behind her suddenly.

Olivia spun to see the clean-shaven face of her father as he came up behind her and scooped her up into his arms. She threw herself around him and felt a swell of relief fill her chest.

"Daddy! I thought I'd missed you!"

"You were running a little behind this time, Peach Muffin. I was afraid I'd missed you, too. I don't think we would've been able to get this big, heavy ship moving because my tears would've kept putting out the fires."

Olivia giggled and squeezed him tight.

"Get to your shift, Ben!" Curly barked. "Captain's going to call for all ahead soon."

"I'm going." Ben Grace said, then squinted at Curly. "You savin' some of that porridge in your mustache for a snack later?"

Curly's hand went self-consciously up to his lip and he fingered his whiskers. A moment later, he turned and ducked back towards the lavatory.

Ben winked at Olivia and she laughed as he gave her one final spin.

"You be safe." Olivia said, just as she always did before every shift. "Don't get burned."

Olivia's father smiled and he replied just as he always did. "No fire can touch Ben Grace. Not while the love of my little Olivia keeps me safe."

She kissed him on the cheek one last time, then he stood up and pulled on the rough, heavy gloves that he wore when he shoveled the coal. She watched him as he walked into the cavernous heat in the belly of the ship. Up above, cooks were preparing the passenger meals and stewards were turning down beds with fresh linens, but Olivia knew that without her father to help push the Carpathia forward, none of those other things would matter at all.

Chapter Two

When Curly had mentioned that Captain Rostron gave Olivia "special treatment", what he had meant was that Olivia was not officially supposed to be on the Carpathia.

After hearing that Olivia's mother had died one year earlier, and when he found out that Ben Grace was her only remaining family, the captain had decided to "make room" for Olivia on the big ship so Ben could continue to work and Olivia could stay near him. That was how, eleven months earlier, the Carpathia had become her home. Since then, Olivia had crossed the Atlantic and back seventeen times.

Mostly, the passengers of the Carpathia were couples or families travelling on holiday. The ship was much more modest than some of the bigger Cunard Line ships that made the Atlantic run, like the Lusitania and the Maurentania, but those who travelled on the Carpathia were often loyal followers of the ship and Captain Rostron. Even so, whenever they left New York, many of the cabins in all classes were unused. It was always much more crowded on the way back to America as immigrants filled the third class, carrying with them everything they owned.

Since the firemen bunks where her father slept were packed four men to a room, Olivia couldn't stay below decks with him (as much as she wanted to), and she also couldn't take a cabin that might have been used by a paying passenger (even if it was sitting empty). The captain had told them to make room for her in the women's crew quarters, where she would have slept on the floor in a tiny room already packed with four teenage girls who worked as stewardesses, but after two uncomfortable weeks of this, Olivia had decided that she needed something much more private.

On the upper decks was a service corridor that connected the infirmary, wireless room, and purser's office. There, in an inconspicuous closet that had been meant for nothing more than to allow repair access to the wiring and plumbing of the ship, Olivia had found her hideaway.

When one first opened the waist-high wooden door, the way was blocked by a maze of pipes and conduits. Undeterred, however, Olivia had crawled beneath this tangle to explore further, and there had found a small space nestled in the back. Here, Olivia had laid out a bed on the metal floor. For the first week, she had slept with only a sheet, but then she had discovered that the laundry room discarded any torn towels and linens that they couldn't repair, so she had smuggled several of them from the discard bin over the months and now had a well-stuffed bed that was softer than most in first class.

There was a service light up in the ceiling, which was always on but never burned too brightly to keep Olivia from sleeping at night. Everything she owned was in a worn and tattered old steamer trunk that had belonged to her mother and also served as a table in her tiny room. The trunk had just barely fit through the tangle of pipes and it had taken her most of a day to work it through to her hidden cubbyhole.

Although she wasn't supposed to be there, most of the crew knew about Olivia's hidden bunk and pretended not to notice. In fact, during the captain's thorough inspection of the ship every Sunday, he would open Olivia's door and peer inside through the tangle of pipes. On more than one occasion Olivia would catch his eye as he peered through at her, then he would stand up and say to his officers *"Boat Deck Service Access 3A- Clear."* before closing the door again and moving on.

After Olivia had changed into some warmer clothes, she combed through her tangle of hair, crouching in front of the tiny, clouded glass mirror that she had propped up on her trunk. The wind from her time in the crow's nest had tied knots in her already unruly locks, and the moist air from the approaching storm had made it frizz into a shocking mess. She pulled the old comb through the thick of it, yanking at the knots until tears welled in her eyes, before finally giving up with a dispirited sigh.

She made her way through the pipes and out the small access door again. The big ship was vibrating more now and Olivia knew that her father was far below shoveling coal as the massive engines pushed them out across the open ocean.

Once out in the corridor, Olivia could hear the rhythmic tapping from the room next door as Harold Cottam, the wireless operator, tapped out Morse code messages on his set. Olivia couldn't help but peek in at Harold, who was bent down low in front of the odd-looking Marconi transmitter with a massive pair of headphones over his ears. The 21-year-old looked flustered as he listened for a response to the signal he had just sent, pressing the headphones harder over his ears.

A moment later, he half-turned and caught her standing in the doorway. A big smile lit up his face (a smile that secretly made Olivia's heart flutter just a bit) and he pulled the headphones down around his neck. "Hey there, Olive Oil!" he greeted her with that charming smile. "What's the word about the ship?"

Olivia shrugged. "Looked like a thunderstorm ahead as we were leaving the harbor." she said.

Harold cringed. "Don't I know it! The interference is killing my signal! It's like trying to hear pin-drops in a cattle stampede. The static is terrible."

"Any interesting messages?" Olivia asked.

Harold motioned with exasperation at the stack of papers nearby. "Not a one. Can you believe this? We're not more than an hour out of New York and people are already sending messages by the trunkload back to the mainland. Complete rubbish like *'Don't forget to feed the cat'* and *'Ask Uncle Freddie to water the roses by the back gate'*. So I'll be working all night to punch through the static back to the mainland just so somebody's garden doesn't wilt while they're on holiday."

"Maybe someday you'll get some big, important message to pass on." Olivia said sympathetically.

Harold laughed. "If I do, Olive Oil, you'll be the first to hear about it!"

Back up on deck, night had fully arrived and the sky was black and starless. On the distant starboard horizon, Olivia could see barrages of lightning snaking through the clouds every few seconds, but that storm was miles away and the captain seemed to be doing a good job of staying clear of it.

Now that they were out at sea, there were no other lights anywhere around them except for the blazing bright electric lights of the Carpathia cutting through the darkness. The black water rolled and swelled down below and would have perilously tossed smaller boats, but the massive passenger liner only swayed gently as she steamed through the night.

Olivia made for the forward stairwell that would lead her to the crew mess hall. She hoped to grab something to eat before they closed up for the evening, but Bubs opened the door before she could get to it and stepped out on deck with her.

"Hey! There you are. You missed dinner!"

"I was on my way down there now." Olivia answered, trying to get past him.

"They already closed up." Bubs said.

Olivia, who hadn't eaten since that morning, threw up her hands in frustration. "What is wrong with me today?" she called out over the wind. "I seem to be two steps behind on everything."

Bubs just shrugged. "Don't worry. Mom saved you some." He pulled out a small bundle wrapped in a linen napkin.

Bubs' parents both worked onboard. His mom was a stewardess and his father worked as assistant purser. Olivia took the package thankfully and settled into an alcove on the deck beside a lifeboat crane. Bubs sat down beside her. Although the wind still whistled around them, they were sheltered from the worst of it.

Olivia unwrapped the napkin to discover a piece of baked chicken, a dinner roll, and an apple. She bit into the roll hungrily. "Tell your mom 'thank you' for me." she said with a full mouth as she chewed.

"It's no problem." Bubs said, hugging his knees up against his chest. Then he added, "The chicken was really good tonight."

Olivia took the hint and tore off a piece of the chicken for herself, then handed the rest of it to Bubs. He bit into it happily.

"So what did you mean that you were two steps behind on everything?" Bubs asked. "Did you miss seeing your dad before his shift?"

Olivia shook her head. "I caught him—just barely. No thanks to that brute Curly Reynolds."

Bubs shuddered. "Ungh. I don't like that guy at all. Hey-- you want to know a secret about Curly?"

Olivia raised her eyebrow at Bubs. "Whaddaya mean? What kind of secret?"

"Well, it's something that I figured out on my own, actually. I think that... well..." Bubs lowered his voice and looked around to make sure nobody was listening. "I think that Curly is actually the devil." he said.

Olivia couldn't help but snort with unexpected laughter and a chunk of the bread that she was chewing flew from her mouth and landed on the deck.

When she was able to swallow again, she nodded in agreement. "He's certainly mean enough."

Bubs shook his head earnestly. "No, no. I don't mean just because he's mean. Think about it... he has a job down below with all of that fire and smoke. Just like you-know-who."

"So does my father." Olivia answered defensively.

"I know, I know." Bubs waved impatiently. "But Curly is in charge. He's the boss down there. And that's not all, either. You know that lump on the side of his head that never goes away? I figured that he had to have a disguise so nobody would recognize him, so he put his cloven hooves into those big old boots he wears, he stuffed his tail down the back of his pants, and his horns... well, he tried to snap them off, but one of them didn't come off all the way, so that's why he's got that big old lump on one side of his head."

Olivia eyed Bubs carefully. "You've really put some thought into this, haven't you?"

Bubs nodded. "Oh, yes. But don't tell anyone else. If he finds out that I know his secret then..."

Olivia smiled and took a bite of her apple. "Don't worry, Bubs. Your secret is safe with me."

A moment later, a flickering light out of the corner of her eye caught Olivia's attention. At first she thought that it was a reflection from the distant lightning storm that she'd seen, but when she looked up, she saw that it was something much, much different.

The ship was on fire.

Chapter Three

Olivia jumped to her feet. "Fire!" she called out, feeling her heart leap in her chest. The long ropes that extended from the crane next to them down to the covered and stowed lifeboat were shimmering an electric blue. Trying to remember the crew drills about what to do if a fire breaks out on the ship, Olivia hesitated for a moment before lunging for the closest door so she could alert an officer.

She was almost to the door when she heard Bubs say with calm fascination "That's not fire… it's St. Elmo's."

Olivia paused with the door half open, the wind throwing her hair furiously around her face. She looked up again at the ropes and saw now that the strange blue glow had crawled up to the metal crane and was starting to spread out along its girders.

"What are you talking about?" Olivia asked, her heart still pounding furiously. "What is St. Elmo's?"

"I saw it once when I was little." Bubs said, watching the growing blue fire in fascination. "It happens during thunderstorms sometimes. It's kinda like electricity."

Olivia watched with alarm as the crane nearby suddenly began glowing bright blue as well, and a long, shimmering line of dancing blue fire started to expand across the ship's railing. She still held the door open in her hands, not sure whether or not to believe Bubs. He had lived on the ship most of his life, though, and he seemed completely calm and enthralled by the expanding blue light around him.

"Is it... dangerous?" Olivia asked cautiously.

Bubs shook his head. "Nah. In fact, it's really good luck to see it. It means that we're going to have a safe voyage."

The eerie silent fire seemed wholly unaffected by the wind and was now expanding up the outer deck railing towards the front of the ship. The massive crane beside them was completely engulfed in the strange blue aura and a bench nearby was beginning to glow faintly. Overhead, a peel of thunder rumbled from the dark sky.

Bubs was looking at the glowing lights around him with an expression of awe. As Olivia watched him, he took several slow steps forward and reached his hand out towards the glowing railing.

"Bubs, don't touch it." she warned. She looked up and down the deck, but didn't see anyone else in sight. She still felt that she should tell someone what was happening.

When Bubs didn't stop moving, she let go of the door and stepped over to him, pulling his hand back just before he reached the railing.

"It not dangerous." Bubs protested.

"Maybe not," Olivia said uneasily. "But it's strange... and I don't like strange."

Just then, there was a buzzing, cracking sound to her right and Olivia spun around to see a new light appear. Beside them, floating about four feet from the deck, a pinprick-sized bright red light bobbed up and down. Its edges danced and shimmered much like the blue light, but this little speck floated and danced in the air like a weaving firefly, not attached to anything.

"St. Elmo's?" Olivia asked Bubs, moving away as the bobbing red light drifted closer.

Bubs bit his lip. "No, that's... um... I don't really know what that is."

Whatever it was, it was still moving closer, and when Olivia moved to the side, the tiny point of red light changed direction and followed. It was definitely making noise, too. While the blue light shimmered all around them in silence, the red light crackled and hissed angrily.

Olivia couldn't help but shiver superstitiously as she recalled their conversation a moment before *"Curly is the devil, but if he found out I knew his secret, then..."*

Bubs was hiding behind Olivia now. The shimmering blue St. Elmo's around them was all but forgotten now as they both watched the approaching red dot warily. When it lurched forward, Olivia scrambled back and almost toppled over Bubs, who was clinging to her tightly.

Then, above the noise of the wind and another deep rumble of thunder from the sky, the shimmering red dot in front of them suddenly spoke.

"How do you do?" it said in a melodic, gravelly voice.

Bubs and Olivia both froze, momentarily horror-struck, then Bubs released Olivia and started running up the deck. Before Olivia could move, though, the red light lunged suddenly at her face. Olivia stumbled back to try to avoid it, but just like everything else that day, she was too slow.

The ghostly red point of light touched the center of Olivia's forehead and in that instant, her mind filled with a booming rush of static and noise. Breaking through the noise came that melodic, gravelly voice again, deafening in its volume. *"BABIES CRY"* it boomed, and then the world was awash with light and Olivia was slumping back against a soft cushioned chair that was somehow rolling backwards with her.

Her body felt numb, as if it had just been dunked in ice water, and her head was spinning. Slowly, the feeling crept back into her arms and legs and she struggled to focus her eyes in the bright light around her. As she blinked, white bursts swam across her vision.

"Whoa, whoa, whoa!" someone was shouting. "Fire! There're a fire over here! Geez, Evie, you blew up your whole computer!"

Olivia could smell the faint acrid smell of electrical smoke, and when she blinked again, she saw now that she was somehow indoors. Bright lights set up high in the ceiling made her squint in their artificial white glare.

Olivia was seated in a rolling chair that was just now coming to a stop and there was a desk in front of her. There was a large computer monitor on the desk that was dark. To Olivia, who had never seen such a thing, it looked like a picture frame that didn't have a picture in it. There was also a computer keyboard, which to Olivia looked like a long, black rectangular tray that was oddly filled with dice, each with a different letter. This was where the smoke was drifting from.

A man rushed up beside her and reached under the desk, pulling an electrical plug out of its socket with a crack of orange sparks. When he straightened up again, Olivia could see that he was a young man in his twenties, with light brown hair and glasses. He was wearing blue jeans and a white coat with a nametag on it.

"Wow, Evie!" he said, looking at Olivia and running his fingers through his hair. "You alright? Geez, look at your hands!"

Olivia looked down at her hands and saw that her fingertips were blackened at the ends. As she wiggled her fingers, she found that they still prickled with numbness. It could have been a trick of the harsh white light in the room, but her hands also seemed oddly different. When she turned her hands over, she was confused to see that her fingernails were somehow painted a bright, glossy red and manicured to

19

an elegant length much like the women she sometimes saw travelling in the first class.

"You've been working the Carpathia feed for ten hours straight." the man continued, shaking his head.

How did my fingernails turn red? Olivia wiggled her fingers again, not understanding what she was seeing. *And... are my fingers longer? They look longer.*

"That's why they tell us to take breaks!" the man was saying. "When you get exhausted, you start making mistakes. When you make mistakes, things happen like your computer blows up in a spectacular way." He turned and looked at the smoking keyboard on the desk with reluctant admiration. "Still, that is absolutely radical. How did you manage to do that exactly? Did you spill some of your Red Bull on it?"

Olivia stared in blank confusion at her surroundings. The man's odd words only made things worse. The nametag on the man's shirt, she now saw, had a blue and white logo that spelled out the word "HistCorp". Instead of the letter "o" in the word, there was a picture of a watchful eye staring out. The name beneath the logo was "Charles Ferryman".

Charles was watching her as if waiting for her to say something. "Hello? Evie? Yoo-hoo. Earth to Evie."

Olivia blinked at him in confusion. "Who's Evie?" she asked, but the voice that came out of her mouth was not her own. It was the voice of a woman.

Charles clapped his hands together. "There she is! I can see that the jolt didn't impair your sense of humor. Still as lame as always." He stood up and started across the small room where there was another desk just like the one near her. "You'd better go report what happened. You know how Dumas gets about these things. She'll probably make you fill out paperwork until you go blind before she'll give you another computer."

The man settled behind his desk and turned back to his own computer. Olivia was startled to see the glass picture frame in front of him begin to flash bright pictures and words that somehow moved and changed as he pressed buttons.

Olivia looked down at herself and saw that she was wearing a white coat much like his and— for some crazy reason— she was wearing blue jeans instead of a proper dress. Craning her head to get a better look, she pulled up the nametag pinned to her own coat and saw the same *HistCorp* logo there, along with the name "Evangeline Deerbourne".

Evie. She thought to herself. *He thinks that I'm someone called Evie.*

Then she caught her own reflection in the dark glass of the monitor in front of her. The dim, hazy reflection looking back at her was a young woman with long, dark hair. Olivia let out a startled cry and her hand went up to her mouth in astonishment.

"I know." Charles said without looking up from his work. "Your keyboard is totally fried. Don't sweat it. It was probably just a power surge or something. If Dumas tries to blame it on you, I'll tell her that it was an 'Act of God' and couldn't have been prevented. Just one of those things."

Olivia got shakily to her feet and immediately her ankle buckled painfully and she stumbled. When she looked down, she saw that her slender black shoes had heels two inches high. When she was finally able to balance herself unsteadily on them, she felt like she was on stilts. It wasn't just the heels, either. She was *way* too high off the ground. She felt nearly twice as tall as normal.

After a few dizzying moments, Olivia walked shakily across the white tiled floor. She stepped out the only door to the room and found herself in a long hallway.

Steadying herself against the doorframe for a moment, Olivia noticed something else immediately. After eleven months aboard the Carpathia, she had grown so accustomed to the ever-present tremor of the engines and the barely-perceptible swaying of the waves that she didn't even recognize them until they were gone.

I'm on land. She thought, and this revelation added another layer to her bewilderment.

The room directly across the hall looked identical to the one she had just stepped out of. Inside were two other people in white coats, both busy at their own workstations. A little sign on the wall just outside the door read "Monitoring room 3285". On the wall beside it was a framed photo with the big "HistCorp" logo along the top of it. The picture showed a family in vivid color (Olivia had never seen a painting that looked so lifelike) and behind them were faded, almost ghostly black-and-white pictures of the pyramids of Egypt, Abraham Lincoln, and a Roman chariot. Beneath the family, in big bold letters, were the words:

HistCorp: We're keeping an eye on our past to make a better future.

None of it made any sense to Olivia. She turned and made her way down the corridor, holding on to the wall for support. Every room she passed was identical to the one she had come from. They were the same all the way to the end, where she turned a corner and found an elevator.

There was a metal plate above the call button with the number "52" on it. She pressed the button with an arrow pointing down and saw it light up. She didn't know what was happening or why, but every instinct in her told her that she had to find a way out of this building right now. Once she was outside, she could see where she was and that was a big first step.

But then the elevator doors opened and bright sunshine suddenly poured over her. Her first, startled thought was that the doors had opened to a sheer drop off the outside face of the building. Then she realized that, impossibly, the elevator itself was made of glass. The outer wall was tinted, and through it she saw the dizzying panorama of a sprawling city from an impossible height... a multitude of glass and steel buildings that seemed to go on forever.

Olivia stood there, frozen, staring out at that astonishing vista. Then the steel elevator doors began to close in front of her and she remained rooted to the spot, still standing in the corridor.

Just before the doors closed, though, Olivia saw something on the horizon that was unmistakable, even in her dazed state.

In the hazy distance, Olivia saw the silhouette of the Statue of Liberty rising over the blue waters of a harbor. Her eyes locked on that lone familiar shape just as the polished steel doors closed again in front of her.

Chapter Four

Those steel doors opened and closed three more times before Olivia found the courage to step into the small glass booth. Without an elevator operator, Olivia wasn't sure she would be able to make it work, but she quickly saw a button labeled with the number "1" and a star beside it, and she pressed it.

She closed her eyes then, holding on to a nearby railing so tightly that her hands hurt. The elevator dropped with a terrifying silent speed that made her stomach twist, and just when the dizzying sensation threatened to overwhelm her, she felt the elevator slide to a stop and the doors opened again.

Warily, she stepped out into a massive lobby. There was a big marble fountain in the center of the room surrounded by flowering trees growing out of massive stone pots. The outer walls were the same tinted glass that had enclosed the elevator and one polished steel wall had a massive "HistCorp" logo sprawled across it, looming above it all.

Five revolving doors were servicing a stream of people both coming in and going out of the building. Four men wearing uniforms stood near some odd-looking arches that people were stepping through to get back towards the elevators where Olivia now stood. Sometimes, one of the guards would take a white paddle and wave it over and around a visitor who stepped through, never touching them with it. While Olivia was watching, the white paddle squealed and the man reached into his pocket and pulled out some keys, dropping them in a nearby bowl. It was all baffling.

Forcing herself to focus, Olivia set her sights on the revolving doors across the lobby and began to walk purposely towards them, careful to keep her balance in the high shoes. As she passed near the uniformed guards, she felt an irrational rush of fear that they would yell out and try to stop her from leaving, but they seemed more intent on watching the people coming in than those going out.

Still, Olivia felt that everyone must be staring at her—like they would somehow know that she was a stranger and didn't belong here. She managed finally to make it to the revolving doors and once she stepped through, she felt a measure of relief to feel the warm sunshine on her face and the rush of city air wash over her.

Olivia began walking through the city that she just barely recognized as New York. There were a few brick buildings like those she knew, but they were dwarfed by impossibly high steel skyscrapers that rose like looming mountains all around her. Instead of the mixed traffic of sputtering automobiles and horse-drawn carriages on the street, people were driving by in steel and glass enclosed cars like she had never seen before. At one point a city bus drove by and Olivia thought that it was a locomotive driving the streets without tracks to guide it.

The mad rush of traffic brought back terrible flashbacks. She closed her eyes as images of her mother's accident welled up in her mind, threatening to tear open old wounds that had only just begun to hurt less. It was only the madness of the situation—the strangeness of it all—that allowed her to push those thoughts back and stay focused on moving forward.

It was eleven blocks later when she first caught a glimpse of the harbor ahead through the buildings. Her ankles were wobbling and crying out in pain, and her feet were blistered and raw. She mostly kept her head down and tried not to look at the menagerie of baffling sights around her. She was relieved, at least, to see some familiar street names as she passed. Although she had never been to this particular part of the city, she knew that it was not supposed to look like this.

When she got to the water, it was almost a relief to be out from between those massive steel buildings. The familiar harbor glittered in the late afternoon sun and massive steel barges floated like giants among a collection of smaller sailboats and tugs. There, out on her little star-shaped island, Olivia saw the Statue of Liberty holding her torch high, just exactly as Olivia had seen her hours before as the Carpathia had sailed past.

Olivia looked out over the horizon, hoping to catch a glimpse of the ship that she called home. Instead, she caught the unnerving sight of a jumbo jet breaking through the clouds overhead.

A flying ship she marveled, and wondered for the fiftieth time if she were dreaming all of this. All that was missing was the white rabbit and she would have been convinced that she had fallen through the looking glass like Alice.

Staring out across the skyline of the city by the harbor, Olivia swallowed and tried to calm the bubbling fear welling up inside of her. Up until now, her only thought had been to make it here to confirm that she had really seen Lady Liberty.

Now that she was here, though, she was more terrified than comforted.

"What's happened to me?" she asked herself, and almost jumped at the sound of the stranger's voice that came from her own mouth. She looked down at her hands again, rubbing her fingers together as if not quite believing that she was actually the one moving them.

She thought—not for the first time—about her father. What had happened to him? What had happened to the Carpathia? "*In fact,*" she wondered as she looked around uneasily. "*What has happened to New York?*"

Olivia patted her white coat where she had felt something weighing it down as she walked. There, from a pocket, she pulled out a small printed wallet. In the opposite pocket she found a cell phone, but had no idea what it was or what it was used for.

Opening the wallet she found some glossy cards of various colors. Some of them had the name Evangeline Deerbourne stamped across their face and one of them had a picture. The picture showed a beautiful, smiling young woman with bright blue eyes and long black hair. Olivia unconsciously reached up and ran a finger through her long hair, pulling some into view to see that it was jet black instead of the normal reddish tangle she was used to seeing.

The wallet also held some money that didn't look exactly like it should, but still had the familiar numbers in the corners and faces of American presidents that she recognized. Olivia was astounded to find seventy-five dollars in all, which was more money than she had ever held in her life. It would have taken her father almost two years to make that much as a fireman on the Carpathia.

"I'm rich." Olivia muttered to herself, and instantly wished that she hadn't as she heard that stranger's voice coming from her lips again.

I'm rich, I'm suddenly a grown woman, and somehow New York City has turned into Wonderland in the few hours since I left it.

Before Olivia stuffed the money back into her wallet, something caught her eye. She held up the cash and squinted at it more closely. There, near the picture of Abraham Lincoln on the five dollar bill were the words *"Series 2025"*.

That was odd because Olivia knew that the series on the bill should have been the year it was printed. Thinking that they must have made a mistake, Olivia thumbed through the other bills and saw that they were all the same. Most were "Series 2025", with one "Series 2024" and one "Series 2022".

Olivia pushed the money back into the wallet, then found the glossy card again with Evangeline's picture.

Eyes: Blue
Hair: Black
Date of Birth: April 30, 1999

Olivia blinked down at the card, then back at the face of the smiling woman in the picture. Her fingers moved up again to touch her unfamiliar black hair and she raised her head to look out at the steel and glass skyline on the harbor.

Then, in the way that only a child's mind is able to grasp and adapt to the unbelievable, Olivia understood in that moment at least a part of what had happened to her.

I'm in the future.

The library on the Carpathia was small but well stocked, and in her eleven months onboard, Olivia had gotten through a good many of their volumes. Along with the more traditional works of Shakespeare and Jane Austen, Olivia had read a book by HG Wells called *The Time Machine*.

Although she couldn't understand why she was in a strange woman's body or how she could have possibly travelled into the future without a machine, Olivia quickly adapted to the strange idea and soon her mind had moved on to trying to decide her next move.

"*Who is Evangeline Deerbourne?*" she asked herself.

After some consideration, the frightful idea came to her: perhaps she really was Evangeline Deerbourne... and had been her whole life. What if, in fact, she only *thought* that she had been a girl named Olivia Grace onboard the Carpathia? What if that was the dream and this was her real life?

Something that the man named "Charles" had said back in that office suddenly came back to her: "*You've been working the Carpathia feed for ten hours straight.*"

The idea was no less strange than the possibility of travelling through time. Had she been born in the year 1999? Was her life on the Carpathia a delusion?

The thought terrified her.

She tried to make herself remember something of her life growing up as Evie Deerbourne, where giant ships with wings flew through the sky and New York was built of glass and steel. She found that she could not recall anything at all from a life like that.

Then she considered all of the clear memories she had of her own life, her father who called her Peach Cobbler and her mother who had always smelled like daylilies...

Still, there was just one way to know for sure if her memories were real or imagined. She looked again at the harbor, then up at the closest street sign which said "West Street". Taking a moment to get her bearings, she started along a path that led along the harbor side through a nearby park. She moved with a purpose again, and that, somehow, made her feel much less afraid.

The sun had gone down and the city around Olivia transformed into a spectacular display of electric lights. They were much brighter than the gas lamps she remembered lining the curbs when she had lived here. Even the few electric streetlights she had seen before were nothing compared to these. When she finally found the small, quiet street where she had once played as a child, she discovered that even this late in the evening it was lit up brightly with high overhanging poles that made it almost as bright as daylight.

The homes here were much older than those closer to the harbor, and many of them Olivia recognized from her own time even though they had undergone some changes over the years. She hobbled past the high, thin brownstone buildings, reading the house numbers until she came to the one she was looking for: #222.

If Olivia had doubted who she really was, those fears were washed away at the first sight of her old home. Immediately, a mixed flood of relief and sadness overcame her, and she stood there under the bright white streetlight for a long moment, staring at the home that she had grown up in, and fighting back the tears that welled up in her eyes.

"I am Olivia Grace." she said to herself in that strange woman's voice. Her memories were real and here was proof.

She moved closer to the house and stepped over the small fence and into the flower garden there. She knelt down beside the stone steps that led up to the front door and ran her hand over them. There, the third step from the top, one of the stones was chipped off in a perfect v-shaped wedge, worn smooth with age. Many of the steps were chipped and weathered now, but when this house was new and these porch steps were otherwise pristine, this one chip in the stone had always bothered her mother. She had chided her father about getting it fixed, and Olivia never thought that she would have been so thankful to find it still broken. After more than 100 years, here was proof that she was Olivia Grace and her memories were real.

Olivia felt the exhaustion overwhelm her then. Her feet were throbbing and her legs were numb. It had been sheer determination that had gotten her here, and now she felt ready to collapse.

With her hand still resting on the chipped step, Olivia curled into a ball and imagined that she was sleeping on the soft pile of linens in her tiny compartment aboard the Carpathia. As she drifted off to sleep, she could almost feel the gentle thrum of the engines and the soft rocking of the ocean waves.

Chapter Five

When Olivia awoke, she felt battered and bruised and sore all over. Her ankles and legs were throbbing, her mouth was dry, and her stomach rumbled hungrily. She blinked awake to bright sunlight, thinking that it was the dim service light that she had been waking up to for the past eleven months and wondering why it was suddenly so bright.

When she opened her eyes, though, everything came flooding back to her, along with her feelings of uncertainty and fear.

Olivia found herself still lying in the flower garden beside the front steps of her old house. Her white coat was filthy and she could feel the cold morning dew soaking through the bottom of her pants. She moved experimentally and winced at the pains from a hundred muscles in her body. Finally, she stretched out her long legs and heard a series of pops and cracks, then reached down to rub her aching feet.

Then, Olivia froze, staring down at the ground beside her with fear and confusion.

The plants and flowers in the flowerbed around her had been pulled up in the night, torn from the ground and tossed into a pile against the stone wall, leaving an exposed patch of bare dirt spread out in front of her. The dirt had been smoothed over again and there someone had scrawled out a message for her in spiky, uneven letters dug into the loose soil.

olivia go to 325 victoria st apt 617

Olivia's heart began to pound as she looked at the cryptic message in the dirt. She pulled herself up and looked around. There were a few cars driving by, some people jogging, an old lady walking her dog—none of them seemed to be paying any special attention to her.

"Someone knows I'm here." Olivia whispered to herself as she stared down at the ground beside her.

Quickly, she rubbed the message out and stepped over the little fence and back onto the sidewalk. Smoothing out her ruffled and dirty white coat, she took one last look up and down the street before quickly hurrying away.

Olivia couldn't help but feel that she was being watched.

The city around her was surging with early-morning traffic, and she imagined that each and every passerby was secretly following her, keeping track of her every move.

She stumbled into one corner of Central Park and, despite the changes, she immediately recognized the place her parents would bring her when she was small. She made a left and followed the winding paths around until she came to the small pond she remembered. There were lots of people jogging here, too, many of them with odd little white plugs in their ears that had wires attached to them. Other people had strange devices hooked around their ears and seemed to be having conversations with someone that Olivia couldn't see. It was all mystifying.

Eventually, Olivia caught sight of a vendor setting up a cart nearby and the smell of fresh hot dogs and polish sausages made her rumbling stomach cry out louder than ever.

She balked when she saw that the hot dogs were selling for $5.00 each. The last hot dog her father had bought her, at a baseball game when she was seven, had cost five cents… and it had been a special treat for her father to have spent that much.

Still, Olivia remembered that she was rich now and pulled out Evie Deerbourne's wallet again. She limped over to the vendor and paid twelve dollars for two hotdogs and a Coca-Cola (which she had never tasted but had always wanted to try). Sitting on a bench near the lake, she devoured every bit of it and the persistent rumbling in her belly finally grew quiet.

She pulled the shoes off of her feet and winced when she saw that her heel had been scraped bloody and raw from miles of walking. She rubbed her strange, slender ankles and noticed for the first time that her toenails had been painted a glossy red just like her fingernails.

She contemplated again the message scrawled in the dirt. Who had written it? Why hadn't they just woken her up and given her the message themselves? It all seemed very sinister to Olivia. She shuddered again to think that someone had crept so close to her while she had slept.

Just then, Olivia's coat pocket began to sing.

"One for the money! Two for the show! Three to get ready now go cat go! Don't you… step on my blue suede shoes!"

The voice coming from Olivia's pocket startled her so much that she let out a scream and started scrambling to pull off the possessed coat. In her struggles, the cell phone in her pocket tumbled out onto the grass in front of her and Olivia

34

saw that it was vibrating and that the ghostly voice and music were issuing from it.

Olivia cringed away from the strange device and noticed as it lay in the grass that the word "Chuck" was flashing across its tiny screen.

Olivia looked around frantically, sure that the singing device would bring unwanted attention to her from the people passing by. Quickly, she snatched the little machine up like it was on fire and tossed it into the pond. Then, looking around self-consciously, Olivia picked up her shoes and ran away quickly in her bare feet across the dew-covered grass.

Taxi cabs were for the rich and affluent when Olivia was growing up. Few ever travelled down her street, but in the heart of the city she had seen many taxis mixed in with the horse and carriage traffic. Now that she was rich (and also because she had no idea where Victoria Street was), Olivia decided that she would give one a try.

About one out of every three cars that passed in the heavy street traffic was bright yellow with "TAXI" printed on its side. Olivia saw a woman step to the curb and raise her hand and one of the yellow cars pulled out of the flow of traffic and stopped for her immediately. With her shoes still in her hand, Olivia did the same and an instant later a taxicab had stopped on the curb in front of her.

Trying her best to look like she knew exactly what she was doing and wasn't scared out of her mind, Olivia slipped into the backseat of the car and an exotic-looking dark-skinned driver turned to face her.

"325 Victoria Street" Olivia said, and before she had finished the last word the car had shot out into traffic again.

It was the most terrifying ride of her life.

Olivia had never moved so fast, and it seemed that the driver darted in and out of the traffic at speeds that would make it impossible to avoid a collision. Several times, Olivia screamed out in horror as the driver changed lanes suddenly, narrowly missing a giant bus that sped by or a person who was trying to cross the street. She clutched the seat with white knuckles and caught a glimpse of the driver watching her through his mirror, his eyebrow cocked like he thought she was crazy.

Eventually, they came to a stop and the driver told her that the fare was $7.00. Again, Olivia was stunned that such a short trip could cost more than a month's worth of her father's hard-earned wages. No wonder only rich people took taxis!

When the taxi had driven away, Olivia found herself on a quiet street lined with big, red-brick apartment buildings. Behind her was a shaded playground where mothers sat chatting with one another as their young children played. A sign on a nearby store said "Subway", but when Olivia peered in expecting to see an entrance to the train line, she instead found that it was a sandwich shop.

The address that had been scrawled in the dirt beside her that morning ended up being the apartments directly across the street. Olivia sat on one of the playground benches and watched the building for a long while, contemplating what she should do.

As much as she distrusted whoever had written that message, Olivia realized that she didn't have much of a choice at this point. The money she had was already going quickly and she knew that she couldn't spend another night out on the street. Whoever had written that message had called her "Olivia", so they must have known that she wasn't really Evie Deerbourne and that meant that they might know a way for her to get back somehow.

Olivia watched as people came and went from the apartment across the street. There didn't seem to be anyone sinister-looking waiting outside and watching for her. She noticed that as people approached the glass front door, they would take a little blue card and swipe it through a slot mounted nearby. Olivia reached into the pocket of her white coat and opened the wallet again. Thumbing through the glossy cards there, she found one that was the same color blue. It had the word "SecurLok" written on one side and a black stripe on the other side.

After watching the people coming and going for a few more moments, Olivia finally stood up and made her way cautiously across the street.

Just as she had seen the others do, she slid the card through the little slot, then pulled on the door. It was still locked. Swallowing nervously, Olivia tried again, but the door remained locked. Getting scared now, Olivia tried one more time, this time with the little black stripe on the card facing the other way. She heard a "click" from the door and snatched it open, stepping quickly inside.

There was an elevator just inside the front door, but Olivia remembered her last experience with an elevator and feared that this one would have glass walls, too. Instead, she stepped into the stairwell and climbed the stairs to the 6th floor. A moment later, she was standing in front of apartment 617.

Olivia tried again to smooth down her filthy and wrinkled clothes, stood up straight, and took a deep, calming breath to try and slow her racing heart. A moment later, she knocked on the door.

She braced herself, ready to meet the person who had left her the cryptic message to come here. After a long moment of silence, Olivia nervously knocked on the door again. She waited again in nervous silence, feeling her heart pounding in her ears. Still, there was no answer.

Olivia leaned in and carefully placed her ear to the door, listening for any sound from the inside. She could hear nothing but her own unsteady breathing in the silence of the hallway.

She looked up and down the corridor, unsure about what to do next. She had been sure that whoever had left her the message would have been here waiting, but now she had a creeping sensation again that she was being led into a trap of some kind.

She started to step away from the door nervously when she noticed that the door handle had the same kind of slot that had been outside the front door of the building. Hesitantly, she reached into her pocket again and retrieved the blue card. She slid it through the slot and heard a faint "*click*".

Taking one last nervous look up and down the empty hallway, Olivia turned the door handle and opened it to reveal a dimly lit apartment foyer.

"Hello?" she called uncertainly into the silence.

Leaving the door open behind her, Olivia stepped inside cautiously, trying to look every direction at once. There was a brass bucket with an umbrella by the door, and a small table with a little machine on it. The number "5" was blinking steadily in red along with a red light beside the words "*New Messages*".

"Hello?" Olivia called again in her grown-woman's voice, taking a few more uncertain steps into the dim apartment.

There was a darkened kitchen on the left and the foyer opened up to a sitting area with a couch and a television (which again to Olivia looked like an oversized photo frame with no picture behind the glass).

Olivia went to the windows and pulled back the curtains, letting sunlight pour into the room. The only other doorway led back to a bedroom with a small bathroom and closet. The apartment was empty and there was no sign of the mysterious messenger who had told her to come here.

Hanging on the wall in the bedroom was a framed photo of a sculpture with the caption "Jeanne d'Arc—Rheims" beside another frame with a tattered and faded postcard addressed to "President Theodore Roosevelt" in flowery script. (*What exactly was he the president of?* Olivia wondered…)

Against one wall, enclosed in a long glass case, was a finely detailed model of a passenger steamship with an unmistakable lone red funnel topped with a black stripe. The plaque in the case simply read "Carpathia- Cunard Line", but seeing it here in this darkened room, in this apartment that she had been led to in this city more than 100 years in the future, sent a superstitious shiver up Olivia's spine.

Olivia turned then and saw several photographs on the bureau. They showed a woman posing and smiling with various people at the beach, a park, in the bleachers of a stadium. Olivia picked up one of the photographs to get a better look, then looked up at herself in the mirror above the bureau and saw the stunned, bewildered expression of the young woman with long black hair looking back at her.

These were pictures of her—or—no, that was wrong.

Not her.

These were pictures of *Evie*. The real Evie Deerbourne.

Chapter Six

Olivia took a bath.

While it was a wonderful, soothing sensation to have the hot water soak away the dirt and grime that covered her and soothe her aching and sore muscles, it was also bizarre to be naked in a strange woman's body. She did her best not to look too often at her reflection in the nearby mirror, but one thing that she couldn't resist was admiring her long black hair as she washed the tangles from it. Her hair was so much softer than the mess of reddish, dry hair that she was used to. This was just the kind of hair that she had always dreamed of having and she enjoyed holding it up into various styles to admire how they looked on her.

The bathtub was draining and Olivia was drying off when she first heard the footsteps in the hallway outside.

They were barely audible at first, but as she strained her ears, she heard the faint squeal of hinges as someone carefully pushed open the bedroom door that she had left cracked.

Olivia's heart jumped and she threw herself against the bathroom door, slamming it closed to keep out the intruder.

Was this the person who had sent the message? Had they arrived now at last? Maybe she had gotten here too early. Maybe they hadn't expected her to come so quickly.

Olivia had left her clothes on the bed in the bedroom and realized now that she had nothing but the towel wrapped around her.

"Who's there?" she called out shakily, straining to hear through the door.

There was a slight creak of floorboards as someone stepped up just outside the bathroom door. Olivia locked it quickly and leaned against it, ready to fight off the intruder if they tried to break through. She couldn't help but imagine the frightful image of Curly Reynolds with his filthy boots and misshapen bald head on the other side of the door, also pressing his ear against the wood to try to hear her inside.

She held her breath, straining to hear, listening tensely for what the stranger would do next. She watched the doorknob, expecting it to move at any moment.

Then, from right outside the door, Olivia heard a plaintive *"Meow!"*

She frowned, and her tense muscles relaxed just a bit.

A moment later, Olivia dropped to her hands and knees and peeked through the crack under the door. There, instead of Curly's soot-covered boots, she saw four furry paws. There was another *"Meow!"* followed by a light scratching as one of the paws lifted to push at the door.

Slowly, Olivia opened the bathroom door and the wide, curious green eyes of a bushy grey cat looked up at her.

"Awww... hey there, kitty!" Olivia said with a smile.

She offered her hand, but instead of coming forward, the cat's eyes widened for a moment as it watched her, then he spun around and darted out of the room.

"Hey! Wait a minute! Come back here." Olivia called, hurrying after it.

Wherever the cat had run to hide, Olivia couldn't find him again.

She found his food bowl on the floor in the kitchen and some cans of food (which had a nifty little metal tab that let her pull open the can without a can opener) in a cabinet. She filled the bowl and tapped it with a spoon.

"Here, kitty kitty!" she called into the empty apartment hopefully, but the cat didn't come back.

"You can tell I'm not your mommy." Olivia said thoughtfully. "I look like her and I talk like her, but you can tell that she's not me."

Olivia had found a dress in the closet and was thankful to be wearing something other than jeans. It had felt so unnatural to be wearing boy clothes. Even so, the most modest dress she could find seemed to be cut way too low in the front, so she found a knit sweater that she pulled on over it.

As she pulled on the sweater, she noticed for the first time a framed certificate above the desk in Evie's bedroom. It was a diploma from Stanford University to Evangeline Elyse Deerbourne. The degree listed was a "Dual-Core Doctorate in History and Quantum Physics". Olivia wasn't sure what all of the words meant, but she was astounded that a woman could graduate from a university. Olivia couldn't recall ever meeting a woman with a degree in anything before and it made her more curious than ever about this strange woman whose body she had somehow stolen.

Her apartment surely showed that she must be as wealthy as she was educated. Although the Carpathia had electric lights, most homes and apartments that she had visited before did not. She was surprised to find that every room in this small apartment had an electric light, as well as several lamps. The sitting room even had an electric fan on the ceiling that was controlled by a switch on the wall.

Before she had switched on the kitchen light, the cabinets and counters had been bathed in a glowing blue light that had reminded her instantly of the St. Elmo's she and Bubs had seen. Closer investigation showed that it was a glowing blue screen set into the door of what she soon discovered to be the icebox. The numbers on the screen somehow changed before her eyes as the seconds ticked by, and the calendar there showed that today was March 8, 2026. Olivia shook her head, running her fingers over the glowing glass screen in amazement.

Inside the icebox, Olivia found some milk (even though the milk was not in the typical glass bottle that she was used to seeing). The carton had the words "Skim Milk" on the side, and Olivia soon discovered that meant it was actually milky water for some reason. Still, she was thirsty, and after drinking the last of it, she opened the apartment door and left the empty carton out in the hallway so the milkman could swap it out when he delivered fresh milk in the morning (although she hoped he brought regular milk this time instead of the watery stuff...)

Olivia found a package labeled "cheese" in the icebox, and it held a stack of thin yellow squares, each wrapped individually with a thin clear paper. She also found a bag that had some bread in it... and the bread was already cut neatly into slices (which Olivia thought was a brilliant idea and was surprised that nobody had thought of selling it like that before). Soon, she had a cheese sandwich. It wasn't quite as delicious as the slabs of creamy cheese between thick slices of hot, fresh-baked bread that she sometimes smuggled out of the Carpathia kitchens with Bubs, but it was enough to satisfy her growing hunger.

Thinking of the Carpathia made Olivia wonder again about her current situation and what she planned to do about it. Someone (who knew she was Olivia) had written her that note in the dirt last night, and it had led her here, to Evie Deerbourne's apartment. If they had planned on meeting her here, something must have stopped them. It seemed important, though, that Olivia wait for them to contact her again. If they knew that she was really Olivia Grace, then they must also know something about what had happened to her.

Olivia ran her fingers through Evie's long black hair again.

If I'm in Evie Deerbourne's body, she thought to herself, *then where is my own body? Did my body somehow change into hers when I came here? Did I age somehow? Is this my own grown-up body? Is this what I will look like when I am older?* Olivia held out a strand of the silky black hair and remembered her own dull reddish hair.

"Definitely not my hair." she muttered. "Wish it was... but it's definitely not."

Then... what?

Is my real body still back on the Carpathia? Is it lying there on the deck, lifeless? Olivia's heart froze at that thought. What if her father thought that she was dead? She couldn't bear to think that. It would be devastating for him, especially so soon after losing mother.

Then, another mind-bending question came to her. *Where is the real Evie Deerbourne? Where is the woman who called this apartment her home? Did we change places? In that instant that I found myself here, did she blink and find herself on the deck of the Carpathia with a twelve-year-old body and tangled reddish hair?*

If that was the case, then right now Evie was probably just as bewildered as she was.

And how exactly did this happen?

Olivia's first thought had been that the strange talking red light that she had seen on the deck of the Carpathia had been a malevolent spirit or fairy that had somehow enchanted her here. Now, though, Olivia wasn't so sure. She thought back to her brief moments at the odd place she had appeared at—

HistCorp. The man there had said that Evie had been watching the "Carpathia feed". It all baffled Olivia, but those had definitely been people and not spirits or fairies in that building.

She mulled over her situation and struggled to make sense of it for the rest of that afternoon. She cautiously explored the apartment, careful not to open anything that looked private. Even though she was in Evie's body, she didn't feel she had the right to snoop. She wondered if Evie was back on the Carpathia right now looking through Olivia's tiny little room. What had she surmised from the things she had found there?

Eventually, the sun dipped below the horizon outside and Olivia decided that whoever was supposed to meet her here wouldn't be coming. She tried not to be too disappointed and decided that at least she would be able to sleep safely in a warm bed that night.

She made one last search for the kitty (who had still not come out to eat his food), then climbed into bed and pulled up the covers. Since Olivia had been sleeping with a light on for almost a year, she soon found that she could no longer sleep in the dark. She turned the bright overhead light on and just before drifting off, she whispered into the empty room. "Goodnight, Daddy. Try not to worry about me. I'm going to find a way to get back to you soon…"

Olivia awoke to an odd noise.

It was a gritty, scraping sound that she tried to ignore. She was so exhausted and just wanted to sleep. The sound was persistent, though, like someone scratching frantically on a wooden door to be let in. A moment later she heard a loud "Meow!" and then the ring of something metallic falling with a loud clatter in the silence.

Olivia jumped up, startled, and found herself somehow seated at a table. It was dark except for a hazy blue glow. After several heart-pounding moments of disorientation, Olivia realized that she was in Evie Deerbourne's kitchen, seated at her table.

In the darkness, the cat was just jumping off the tabletop. As she watched his shadowy silhouette, he scampered to his food bowl and began eating. A low, rumbling purr issued from his throat as he dug in.

Olivia did not remember coming into the kitchen. She blinked her tired eyes and saw that the glowing blue screen on the icebox door said that it was 2:34 a.m. She frowned and turned to see that the light from the open bedroom door still glowed brightly.

When she moved to stand, her hand brushed against something on the table, knocking it to the floor.

In confusion, Olivia clicked on the kitchen light. She saw that it was a fork that had fallen. It lay on the floor beside the table and... strangely... its tines were bent and twisted out of shape.

Olivia moved to pick it up, but before she could bend down, she saw something that made her breath catch in her throat.

The smooth surface of the kitchen table was covered in a scatter of fresh wood shavings and Olivia's realized with a jolt that a message had been gouged there in the wood in the same spiky, uneven lettering that had been scrawled in the dirt the night before.

This time the message read:

olivia get help i am trapped in

The final letter of the message was only half formed and it looked as if whoever had written it had been interrupted.

Immediately, Olivia ran to the door of the apartment and checked it. It was still locked with the chain latched firmly in place. Still, she unlatched it and peered into the hallway outside. It was clear in both directions (and her empty milk carton was still there).

She closed the door again and refastened all of the latches. She turned back toward the empty apartment and immediately switched the lights on.

"Hello?" she called out shakily, her mouth dry. "Is anybody in here?"

There was no answer. To be safe, Olivia pulled a big knife from one of the kitchen drawers and made a thorough check of every room and every closet, looking under beds and into any space or corner that a person could hide.

Eventually, satisfied that she was alone, she ended up again in the kitchen, staring down at the terrifying message carved into the table. She reached down and picked up the bent and twisted fork and looked at it closely. When she looked up, the cat was there by his empty food bowl, licking his lips and looking up at her.

Olivia looked into his green eyes and a superstitious shiver snaked up her spine. She swallowed and looked at him nervously.

"Did you do this?" she whispered, frightened, into the silence of the kitchen.

The cat just stared back at her wordlessly.

Chapter Seven

Olivia couldn't sleep for the rest of that night. She sat on the couch with the lights on and her knees curled up against her chest, jumping at every sound she heard. The big kitchen knife lay on the table nearby.

She couldn't help but wonder again if maybe spirits or fairies *were* to blame for all of this somehow. She no longer thought that it was an ordinary person who had been writing the messages to her. Unfortunately, all of the remaining possibilities were each more terrifying than the last.

This latest message definitely had a sense of urgency to it. "*Get help*" it had said, but where was she supposed to get help... and who exactly needed help? Did she need to find help for herself or for the person writing the message?

Part of her wondered if it was Bubs.

He had run away just before she had been zapped here, but maybe something had happened to him, too. "*I'm trapped in...*" the message had started to say before it had been interrupted. Was Bubs trapped somewhere and needed her help? Where?

I'm trapped in...

... in what exactly?

Just then the cat reappeared and jumped up on the coffee table in front of her. It stood and watched her silently for a long moment.

I'm trapped in the cat's body? Could that have been the message? Maybe Olivia had been thrust into Evie Deerbourne's body and Bubs had found himself inside a cat, unable to talk.

Olivia stared meaningfully into the cat's eyes. "Bubs?" she asked gravely. "Is that you?"

The cat didn't answer, and a moment later he seemed to lose interest in her and wandered off into another room.

"You're being ridiculous." Olivia muttered to herself.

She turned and looked at the predawn light streaming in from the window. Olivia knew that she couldn't hide in the apartment forever. Sooner or later, she was going to have to get out there and find a way to help herself if she ever hoped to get back to her father. She just wished she understood more about what was happening.

Olivia thought about the city outside and it made her uneasy to even think of going back out there. She may as well have been on another planet. The future had transformed the New York that she had known all of her life into something incomprehensible.

"I've got a hundred and fourteen years of catching up to do." she said to herself... and that was when she realized what her next move would have to be.

On May 24, 1911, the main branch of the New York Public Library on Fifth Avenue was opened to the public, and

Olivia Grace was there. It was one of the last things she had done as a family with both her mother and her father... two weeks before her mother's accident... and Olivia remembered sitting atop her father's strong shoulders and looking over the heads of the massive crowd at the two majestic stone lions that crowned the library's front steps.

Now, Olivia stood staring up at those lions in this strange and transformed city. They were just exactly as she had remembered them, and as she stood at the bottom of those steps, she could almost hear the sounds of the gathered crowd still ringing in her ears over the distance of more than a hundred years.

Olivia soon found that the inside of the library had not remained as unchanged as those lions after a century. There were no catalogs to thumb through to find books. Instead, there were rows upon rows of those machines with the glowing screens and dozens of people staring at them intently as they typed away on the keyboards.

Feeling altogether intimidated, she was relieved to see a sign with the words "Help Desk" over in the corner. She nervously approached the woman there and asked where she could find some books about history.

"You'll need to be more specific than that." the woman said politely.

"Um... the last 100 years or so." Olivia said.

The woman cocked her eyebrow at Olivia. "Okay. Any specific event?"

Olivia bit her lip. "Do you have anything that's sort of like an overview of... everything?"

"An overview of everything?" the woman repeated.

"Um hmm."

"World, Europe, Asia, America...?"

"Oh... um... I suppose I'll just start with America if that will help narrow it down."

The woman smiled. "Let me see what I can dig up."

It was less than fifteen minutes later that Olivia was presented with a sizeable book called "America and the 20th Century: A Look Back."

Olivia settled into a reading nook and took out the pad of paper and pencil that she had brought with her from Evie's apartment. Opening the book, she saw that it was divided into sections by decades. To save time, Olivia skipped ahead to the mid-1910's and began reading.

She was shocked to see something terrible immediately. In just a few short years, the world would be torn apart by a war unlike any ever seen. They called it "World War I" (Olivia was alarmed by the numeral "I". How many of these great wars were there that they could only keep track of them by numbering them? It certainly made her uneasy about continuing with the pages ahead...)

Olivia shuddered as she saw the pictures and read about one massive battle after another. It seemed unfathomable that the time she had come from was on the brink of something so devastating.

Reading on, she saw that alcohol was banned in the United States in the 20's and read about the economic collapse that led to the Great Depression of the 1930's. In the 1940's, another immense war (number "II") covered the entire world and ended when the United States dropped a new bomb on two cities in Japan. The 1950's was an era of optimism and a new kind of music called "Rock and Roll" and (this amazed Olivia) in the 1960's people actually left the Earth and travelled to outer space and walked on the moon. The 1970's were riddled with social change and more wars and in the last part of the 1900's, technology grew by leaps and bounds... transforming the way almost everything was done. In these sections, she learned about computers and cell phones and the internet.

When she was finished reading four hours later, Olivia sat back and stared in awe at the still-blank notepad in front of her. She was born in 1899 and she felt as if she had just read the history of her entire life in the space of a few hours. It was a disorienting and somewhat terrifying feeling to know what was in store for the world.

When Olivia stepped out of the library again and into the bright afternoon sunshine, she looked at the city around her with new understanding.

She had a massive slice of pizza and a Coca Cola for lunch, sitting on a bench across from the stone lions and mulling over the one hundred years of history that she had consumed. After sitting there for a long while, dazed and overwhelmed, she finally made herself get back up and go inside again.

This time, Olivia eyed the rows of machines that she now understood to be computers. She stood back and watched a few people using them and finally decided to try it herself.

She found an empty workstation and pulled up her chair. In front of her on the screen, a small vertical line blinked on and off inside a box. Experimentally, Olivia tapped a letter on the keyboard and saw the letter appear on the screen in the box.

Neat.

Olivia had already decided what she needed to research. If, in fact, she was able to get back to the Carpathia and live out her life, then there might be something about her and what she does in her lifetime. Maybe she was in the history books herself somehow.

Carefully she typed in the words "Olivia Grace" and then crossed her fingers.

C'mon. Let me be either a famous actress or a famous author.

She hit the "Enter" key.

```
Search: Olivia Grace
Relevant matches: 0
```

Olivia frowned. *Well, that can't be good.*

She bit her lip thoughtfully, then typed in her next search.

Search: Ben Grace
Relevant matches: 0

Well, all right. Olivia thought to herself. *So my dad and I aren't famous enough to be in the history books. So what? That doesn't necessarily mean anything.*

Olivia decided to try something different.

Search: Carpathia
Relevant matches: 5007

Wow. That's more like it.

Olivia clicked on the first match and was amazed to see a photograph of her familiar ship appear on the screen. She couldn't help but smile.

She read about the Carpathia from its beginnings in the shipyards to its time with its most remembered captain, Arthur Rostron. Olivia smiled again as she looked at a picture that showed the familiar smiling face of the kind captain.

Her smile quickly disappeared, though, as she read on.

The Carpathia is, of course, most famous for its frantic race to rescue the survivors of the doomed ocean liner RMS Titanic, which sank after striking an iceberg on the night of April 14, 1912, taking the lives of over 1,500 passengers and crew in the most tragic event in maritime history.

Olivia blinked at the computer screen in stunned silence. A numbing cold crept into her chest as she read over the passage again.

The Titanic.

She knew the ship, of course, just as most of the world did in her time. She was the crown jewel of the White Star Line and touted as the biggest and most luxurious ship in the world. Olivia remembered reading about the Titanic embarking on her maiden voyage just a few days before, and had overheard even some of the Carpathia crew whispering about the massive ship with grudging envy.

Olivia shivered again as she noticed the date.

April 14, 1912.

That was just three days from the night the Carpathia had sailed out of the harbor. It was going to happen on that very crossing.

Olivia couldn't even imagine one thousand five hundred people dying at one time. To her, it was more horrible and shocking than anything she had read that day. While all of the other wars and atrocities had seemed surreal and distant, this was something that was almost personal to her.

Olivia's fingers hovered over the keyboard for an uncertain moment, then she began typing again.

```
Search: RMS Titanic
Relevant matches: 786,925
```

Olivia clicked on the first match and began to read.

Chapter Eight

Seven hours later, Olivia had completely filled the front and back of every page in the legal pad she had brought from Evie's apartment and she had sharpened her pencil so many times that it was now half the size it had been that morning.

She had notes about the Titanic's fatal collision with the iceberg and an exact timeline—down to the nearest minute— of every event that led up to and followed that fatal moment.

She read about Carpathia's dash through the night as the massive liner sank, only to arrive hours too late to find just 700 near-freezing survivors floating in scattered lifeboats at dawn. She read about the heroic actions of Captain Rostron and the key role that wireless operator Harold Cottam played as he picked up the Titanic's desperate midnight call for help. She knew about the positions of the Carpathia and the Titanic, and even the smaller ship *Californian* who, unknowingly, sat within sight of the sinking ship on that dark night.

For Olivia, though, the pictures were the worst. There were pictures of the lifeboats approaching the Carpathia at dawn and pictures of the huddled and freezing survivors on the deck, being tended to by members of the crew. They all looked so stricken by what they had been through and what they had seen. Olivia recognized several people in the pictures, and in one she even saw Bubs as he handed a cup of hot coffee to a woman wrapped in blankets. He was unmistakable, even in the grainy and faded picture. (*So you're still safe and sound back where you should be, Bubs. Maybe that means you didn't get zapped along with me after all.*)

She found herself reaching out to touch the computer monitor, longing to jump in there somehow and be back on the deck of the Carpathia with them. Even after closely scanning every picture she could find, though, she never once saw herself standing among the huddled survivors.

The pictures made tears well up in her eyes... partly because she so desperately missed her home and the people she loved, and partly because the tragedy of the Titanic was the most terrible thing she could have ever imagined.

Later, she saw pictures that had somehow been taken of the Titanic as she lay encrusted in coral at the bottom of the sea. These pictures had been too much for Olivia to bear, and she had moved past them quickly, fighting back tears.

By the time it was getting dark and the library was closing, Olivia felt physically and emotionally exhausted. She was nodding off even as her hand jotted down every note, fact, and figure that she could consume.

Finally, after actually falling asleep for a solid few minutes, Olivia shook herself awake and decided that she had better go. Reluctantly, she pulled herself up away from the computer and headed back to Evie's apartment.

The empty milk carton was still outside of the apartment door, and a sour odor had begun to fill the hallway. Olivia wondered why the milkman had not come that morning, and decided that she would leave it out one more night to see if he had just overlooked her that day.

Once inside Olivia fed the cat (who now came up to her and brushed her legs in welcome) and she gave him a friendly scratch behind the ear, whispering to him with a smile "Did you have a good day, Bubs?" (She no longer believed that the cat was actually Bubs, but she had decided that it was as good a name for him as any.)

Olivia changed for bed and closed and locked the bedroom door. She pulled herself under the covers with the bright light on overhead and a hundred years of history still swirling in a chaotic jumble through her mind. She began thumbing through her massive stack of notes on the Titanic and noticed with wry amusement that her handwriting got progressively worse as the hours had gotten later. In fact, near the end of the notepad, it was almost illegible in some places, dropping off the side of the page at one point as she had dozed off in mid-sentence.

Then, when Olivia turned the page, she saw something that made her sit upright suddenly in the bed.

There, impossibly, another message had been written in the same spiky, jittery lettering as the two messages she'd found the nights before. This time, the ominous message appeared in the middle of a sentence that she had been writing—the handwriting changing suddenly to the bold, dark handwriting of the stranger.

i am here olivia i am evie i am trapped inside here with you we need to get help

Olivia stared at the note, both scared and confused by it.

I am Evie...

It was Olivia's hand that had written this. Somehow, maybe in a moment of exhaustion as she had been nodding off in the library, her own hand had scrawled out that spiky message.

But it's not really my hand, is it? Olivia thought with a chill, and she lifted her grown woman's hand and flexed her manicured fingers.

It's Evie's hand.

Olivia read the message again.

I am trapped inside here with you.

What did she mean? Trapped inside where?

With you...

Did she mean that she was inside... her body?

Maybe Evie Deerbourne didn't really go anywhere when I arrived. Olivia thought to herself with growing alarm. *Maybe I just sort of shoved Evie aside when I got here. Maybe Evie is still trapped in this body somewhere, watching and helpless until...*

"Until I fall asleep." Olivia whispered into the empty room.

Olivia looked down at the spiky message again and an involuntary shudder coursed through her. There had been a woman on the Carpathia about six months earlier who had claimed that she could go into a trance and write messages from dead people. She claimed that the spirits took control of her hand as she wrote.

Of course, the magic of Harry Houdini had made those sort of things popular the last few years—especially with rich people who were always looking for something to amuse themselves with. Olivia's mother used to scoff whenever she read about it in the papers. "People will always find new and ridiculous ways to throw away their money." she would say.

This lady aboard the Carpathia had been something different, though. There had been something... dark... about her, and Olivia had felt a cold chill whenever the woman looked at her. One afternoon Olivia had passed her on the deck and without warning the woman spoke up and said that she could contact Olivia's mother from beyond the grave for her. Olivia had instantly refused, horrified at the very thought of the idea, but even as she hurried away, the woman called after her "Beware of the tower on the 3rd of May!"

It was all nonsense, of course, but it had given Olivia the creeps nonetheless.

This was different from the spirit-guided writing that woman had claimed to do. She knew that. She tried to soothe her unsteady nerves by again reassuring herself that what was happening to her was NOT the work of spirits. Still, though, she found herself reluctant to try what she knew she had to do next.

Olivia got up and walked over to the desk in the corner of the room, where she retrieved a clean pad of paper. She climbed back into the bed and laid the pad beside her, taking a deep, slow breath and trying to make herself calm down. She held a pencil loosely in her hand and relaxed as completely as she could, letting the tip of the pencil rest against the paper. It took several moments before she could will her hand to stop trembling.

"I'm going to try to let you write, Evie." Olivia said out loud, feeling a little scared and a little foolish for talking to the empty room. "If you are still inside your body somehow, try to move the pencil and let me know."

Olivia relaxed and tried to clear her mind completely. She focused on making her writing hand as limp as possible. She took slow, deep breaths and tried to control her heartbeat, which was racing furiously at the moment.

For a long time, nothing happened.

Olivia considered that it was possible that Evie may not be able to do anything until she was actually asleep, but then just as she was about to give up, her hand seemed to jerk involuntarily and the pencil scratched an uneven mark across the clean paper.

Olivia jumped and withdrew her hand quickly, her heart pounding so hard now that she felt it might burst through her chest at any moment.

Closing her eyes and struggling to get a hold of herself, she finally lowered her hand against the paper again and closed her eyes, taking deep, uneven breaths.

The long silence stretched out.

Then…

When her hand jumped again, Olivia bit her lip, but kept her eyes closed and willed her arm to stay relaxed. She heard the scratching of pencil against paper, and when the sound stopped, she warily opened her eyes and saw that words were scrawled across the clean paper in spiky, uneven lettering.

i am here

Olivia tried to swallow but her mouth was suddenly bone-dry. She cleared her throat. "Evie?" she asked.

There was a long moment of silence, then the scratching of the pencil again.

Yes

Olivia stared at the word on the page and struggled to come to terms with everything that it meant. After one shocking revelation had followed another that day, she suddenly found that this last was just too much to take in. Without realizing what was happening, Olivia's vision began to tunnel and she felt herself falling against the pillows before everything faded to black.

Olivia's eyelids fluttered awake to predawn morning light seeping in through the slats of the blinds. A furious headache pounded against the inside of her temple and for a long time she lay there, awake but not yet willing to move.

When she finally did turn over, there was a rattle of paper and when she reached beneath herself, she pulled out the crumpled writing pad from the night before.

Olivia looked at the writing there and her headache pounded more painfully than ever.

I am here. It said. *Yes.*

But it seemed that Evie had continued writing after Olivia had passed out. There was more now. A lot more. Olivia held the pad up in front of her and tried to rub the sleep from her eyes as she squinted at the newly scrawled message.

i do not understand how this has happened any more than you do i don't even know who you are i just heard you say your name olivia grace that first night

who are you? you seem just as lost and confused about all of this as i am

Olivia stared at the message and rubbed her pounding forehead. She took a deep breath and spoke again into the empty room. "I'm twelve years old and the only thing that I've been able to figure out so far is that I've somehow come 115 years into the future. Three nights ago I was sailing out of the New York Harbor aboard the Carpathia on April 11, 1912. Then—*zap!*—I'm somehow a grown woman named Evie Deerbourne."

Olivia sat in the silence of the room for a long moment, then reluctantly turned to a new page in the writing pad and picked up the pencil again, holding it limply in her hand against the paper.

There was a long pause, but Olivia got the sense that it wasn't that Evie was struggling to try to write, but that she was trying to decide what exactly to say.

Finally, the pencil began moving.

i was monitoring the carpathia when something happened to my workstation

Olivia closed her eyes against the pounding in her head and took a deep breath. "I don't know what any of that means, Evie." she said. "But whatever happened, I want this to be over just as much as you do. I need to get back. Something terrible is going to happen and I need to try to stop it if I can."

Again, there was a long pause before the reply came.

now I understand why you were reading all of those things in the library yesterday... and now I wish that you had not

this complicates things so much more

we need to get back to HistCorp

the answer to undoing all of this is back there

Olivia thought back to the sinister-feeling building with its terrifying glass elevator and she shuddered. "What is that place, anyway? What were you doing there?"

look in my desk——third drawer down on the left

there is a clear case there with a silver disk in it

Olivia dutifully got up and opened up the desk drawer as instructed. Inside was a case with a silver disk. The disk had the words *"HistCorp public informational video"* printed across it.

now insert the disk into the box beneath the television and play it

After her reading yesterday, Olivia knew what a television was and knew that in her hand she held a DVD. She walked into the next room and put the disk in, then... with an inexplicable sense of foreboding, she reached out and carefully pressed the button marked "Play".

Chapter Nine

The screen on the wall lit up to show the big, bright HistCorp logo with the creepy, watchful eye in the center. Classical music began to play, and a moment later an older woman appeared on the screen wearing the familiar white lab coat that Evie had been wearing that first day.

"Hello. My name is Minerva Dumas and I am the founder of The History Corporation—or HistCorp for short. Our public relations department has put together this informational video to help meet the overwhelming public curiosity about our unique and well—world-changing services. Although our work is heavily steeped in complex quantum physics, this simplified overview should give you a better understanding of who we are and what HistCorp is doing to make our world a better place. I hope you enjoy."

At this point, the video faded out and a montage of historical pictures appeared, along with a man's solemn voiceover. "Mankind looks toward the future, guided by the lessons of history past. What is history, though? The history we know is not necessarily the true record of events as they happened. Winston Churchill said that 'history is written by the victors'. The emperors and conquerors of our past have twisted and molded history for their own purposes and glorification, often erasing the truth to ensure their own spotless legacies. The written histories of the world are whitewashed or one-sided or—in many cases—altogether made up."

"So how can we know the truth? How can we know what really happened? At HistCorp, we've found a way. Using the very latest in quantum research and technology, we are able to watch history as it actually unfolds, recording the true words and events as they happened."

Then, startlingly, the picture on the screen changed. It showed hazy, featureless silhouettes of a crowd of people. They were nothing more than a ghostly grey, shifting blur on the television, but they were unmistakably arranged in rows, like a seated audience. The whole image bobbed and weaved as if the cameraman where balancing on a rocking boat.

The sounds that accompanied the disturbing image were muffled, as if underwater. As Olivia listened she could hear the warbled melody of indistinct music drifting through. The caption at the bottom of the screen read- **"Ford's Theater, April 14, 1865, 10:15:22pm**."

The seconds were ticking ahead.

Then, as the music came to a close, there was some commotion in the top left corner of the screen. There was a bright flash, then a single woman's scream—chilling as it broke through the ghostly static. The music stumbled to an uneven stop and someone yelled out above the murmur of the shimmering crowd "The President has been shot!"

The picture cut then to an image of Abraham Lincoln and the narrator continued. "This extraordinary archive footage is one small sample from a vast and growing library of newly-documented historical events made possible by the scientific breakthroughs of our researchers at HistCorp. In the few short years since we have begun, we have astonished scholars worldwide with remarkable and never-before-known details about world-changing events such as..."

"...the fate of the settlement of Roanoke,"

"...the final moments of Amelia Earhart,"

"...the catastrophic event that triggered the extinction of the dinosaurs,"

"...and the birth and crucifixion of Jesus Christ."

Each event that the narrator called off was accompanied by the flash of another hazy and indistinct grey-colored image showing one startling revelation after another. Olivia stared in open-mouthed awe at the screen, unable to believe what she was seeing and hearing.

"But how is this possible?" the narrator asked, echoing Olivia's very thoughts. "Well, this all came about through a series of remarkable breakthroughs in quantum physics early in the 21st century... after scientists were able to prove the existence of theoretical 'wormholes' in time and space. Contrary to hypothetical speculation, these miniature, molecular-sized tunnels through time were not at all rare. In fact," the narrator chuckled, "our world is absolutely riddled with them, each of them leading to a different time and place! Scientists were amazed to discover that, in a single cubic meter, there may be as many as two billion of these invisible little tunnels moving over, under, and even through you without you ever knowing it!"

An animation appeared on the screen showing a family sitting at a kitchen table, happily eating dinner while blissfully unaware of clouds of little red dots that swarmed all around them. Olivia shuddered and sank back into the couch cushion, looking warily at the empty living room around her.

"Using an advanced form of particle reflection, scientists are able to send a stream of specially charged energy through these wormholes and then reconstruct an image and audio based on the way the energy is reflected back-- kind of like radar with a soundtrack! In this way, we can peek through these tiny little tunnels to see what's on the other side."

The picture showed a cartoon man in a white lab coat straddling up to a wormhole and peering into it with a big goofy grin like it was a telescope.

"Of course, out of billions of wormholes, nearly every one leads only to the empty blackness of outer space, or the interior of a mountain, or overlooks nothing at all of historical value."

The cartoon scientist frowned as he looked through the wormhole at a slug crawling along the ground. The animated slug smiled at the camera and shrugged sheepishly.

"With the help of modern supercomputers, though, we have been able to more quickly sort through them and find the tunnels that do lead to something worthwhile... so we can identify and record what we find for the betterment of the entire human race."

At that moment, the music swelled to a moving crescendo and Minerva Dumas appeared back on the screen in her white lab coat with a satisfied smile on her face.

"As you can see, what we are doing at HistCorp is nothing short of... well... historic. By better understanding our true past, we can shape a more perfect future for ourselves and generations to come."

The screen then faded to the blue HistCorp logo again, this time with the tagline along the bottom. The narrator read it out loud in a soothing voice. "HistCorp—Keeping an eye on our past to make a better future!" After the screen went black, Olivia continued to stare at it for a long time.

Her headache was gone.

She walked back into the bedroom and retrieved the pad and pencil, trying not to imagine that she was walking through a swarm of invisible wormholes. Eventually, she sat down at the kitchen table and dropped the pad on top of the message that Evie had carved into the tabletop the night before last.

Olivia struggled to comb through the jumble of thoughts in her mind to make sure she understood what she had just seen. Up until yesterday, she hadn't even known what a helicopter was and now she was struggling to understand quantum physics.

"All right," Olivia said out loud to the empty kitchen. "So... let me make sure I understand this. There are tiny little pinprick-sized holes in the air all around us that are like little tunnels? Is that right?"

The pencil started moving immediately.

right

"And these tunnels, even though one end comes out into your kitchen right now, the other end of the tunnel might come out in one of the pyramids of Egypt four thousand years ago?"

correct

Olivia considered this. "That's just weird." she said.

yes it is weird Evie agreed.

"So, when you said that you were 'monitoring the Carpathia', does that mean that you were peeking through one of those little tunnels at me?"

yes Evie answered.

Olivia remembered back to that night on the deck with Bubs and one more piece of the puzzle fell into place. "I think I saw your little wormhole thingy." Olivia said thoughtfully. "It was glowing red."

Thats not possible

Olivia laughed. "I am sitting here one hundred years in the future, inside someone else's body, having a conversation with my hand who is writing back to me... and you still want to say that something is not possible?"

Sorry

youre right

Olivia grinned at the absurdity of their situation, then chewed her lip thoughtfully. "When you said that we needed to get help, did you have someone in mind? Were you planning on going to this Minerva Dumas lady or something?"

Evie's response was immediate and the pencil pressed into the paper more forcibly than before: *NO! we cannot let dumas know that this has happened*

Olivia frowned. "Why? What's wrong with Dumas?"

cant trust her

Olivia considered this. "Well then… who?"

need to get to chuck

"Is that the guy you were working with when the computer fried? Charles Ferryman?" Olivia asked.

yes

"And you think he might be able to undo this? To get me back into my own body?"

i dont know

"You said you can't trust this Dumas lady. Can you trust Mr. Ferryman?"

i think so

Olivia twisted her mouth as she looked down at the paper in front of her. "I would have rather you said 'definitely yes'" she muttered, to herself, then took a deep breath. "Is there anything else you think I need to know before we dive into this?"

The pencil scratched across the paper.

natasha cutiepeepers

Olivia looked at the odd message and wrinkled her nose. "What?"

The pencil continued.

the cat

her name is natasha cutiepeepers

Chapter Ten

Evie's HistCorp uniform was filthy and wrinkled from Olivia's night curled up in the flowerbed, so Olivia was introduced to the wonders of the laundry room in the basement of the apartment building. In less than an hour, the white lab coat was mostly white again.

Back at the apartment, Olivia took her time brushing through her long black hair for what may be the last time. She looked at Evie's beautiful face in the mirror and couldn't resist opening up the makeup case on the counter. Although she had seen rich women in New York and aboard the Carpathia who painted their faces beautifully with the latest cosmetics from Paris, she had never gotten a chance to try it herself. Most of the items in the makeup case were mysterious and exotic to her, but she at least recognized the eye liner and blush and applied both heavily. Then she found some lipstick and carefully painted her lips a bright red.

When she was finished, she looked in the mirror at Evie's face and frowned. Instead of looking like a beautiful, wealthy young woman, she looked remarkably like a circus clown. Evie must've agreed because when Olivia looked down, she had used her hand to scrawl across the countertop with the lipstick she still held.

wash it off

Olivia didn't argue.

When Olivia stepped into the big glass-walled lobby of the HistCorp building, she immediately felt that sense again that her every move was being closely watched.

People moved all around her... many of them also wearing the white HistCorp coat like Evie's. She blended right in, yet as she passed the big central fountain she felt like she was in a spotlight and that people must sense that she didn't belong there.

She approached the guard's station without stopping and, just as Evie had told her, presented her HistCorp ID card to the uniformed officer there.

He smiled at her. "Good morning, Ms. Deerbourne."

Olivia considered the guard. Black, curly hair. Mustache. This was the one named...

"Good morning, Marty." Olivia smiled.

"We haven't seen you in a few days." Marty said. "Have you been feeling alright?"

"Better now, thank you Marty." Olivia stepped through the metal detector and soon was past the guard station without incident.

"Have a good day, Ms. Deerbourne."

"Thank you. You too."

Then Olivia was at the elevator door and letting out a slow, relieved breath. She was amazed that people actually thought that she was a grown up and she felt remarkably proud of herself for having pulled it off so well.

The doors opened and she stepped inside with several others who were also wearing white coats. Some of them smiled at Olivia and she nodded and smiled back, just like a proper young woman should. As they rose, she kept her eyes fixed purposely on the numbers above the door instead of the glass walls around her and the terrifying vista beyond. When the flashing display finally settled upon the 52nd floor, Olivia once again smiled and nodded to the remaining passengers and stepped out, forcing herself not to betray the nervous fear that threatened to overwhelm her.

She walked down the long hallway until she came to the door marked "Monitoring Room 3284" and inside she found Chuck Ferryman sitting at his workstation and cycling through a number of hazy grey images like the ones she had seen in the informational video. She also saw that Evie's workstation had been replaced and there was a new one waiting for her.

Chuck looked up at the door, saw her standing there, and did a double-take. "Well look who decided to come into work today! My prodigal partner! Where in the name of great Odin's beard have you been, Evie? You're gone for days, you don't return my calls... you know that Dumas is about ready to give your job away."

"Sorry, I've been sick." Olivia said, then cut a glance up to see the security camera watching them from the back corner of the room, just where Evie had said it would be.

Chuck pushed his glasses up with an exasperated gesture. "That's it? You couldn't call in to let someone know?"

Olivia recited the lines then that Evie had made her memorize. "The doctor said that the electrical shock I received when my workstation overloaded must have induced a temporary frontal lobe dementia."

Chuck blinked. "Seriously? You got amnesia? That is so wicked cool. I've always wanted to get amnesia."

"Maybe you have before but just don't remember." Olivia ad-libbed.

Instead of laughing at this, Chuck seemed to seriously consider the possibility. "Wow. I guess that's true…"

Olivia remembered the plan that she had worked out with Evie and carefully cleared her throat. "Um… Chuck. How about we go out for lunch today?"

Chuck had already turned back to his workstation and was flipping through images again. "Sure. Alright. That pizza place off Time's Square?"

"That's the one." Olivia nodded.

When Chuck didn't respond, she cleared her throat anxiously and cut another nervous glance towards the watching security camera in the corner.

"Chuck?" Olivia prompted.

"Yes Evie dear?" Chuck answered without looking up.

"I'm hungry now."

Chuck stopped then and blinked at her, then cut his eyes up at the big clock on the wall. "It's nine thirty in the morning."

"The pizza will be fresh. We'll beat the crowds."

He cocked his eyebrow at her. "Are you serious?"

Olivia nodded and took him by the arm. "I'm serious. Let's go."

Chuck continued to stare at Olivia as if she had lost her mind, but he didn't say anything else until they were out of the building and half a block away. They were passing an alley when Olivia caught sight of an old, dirty sandwich shop sign.

"Down here." Olivia said, and led the way, looking around for any sign that they had been followed.

"This isn't the pizza place!" Chuck protested.

"I changed my mind." Olivia said tersely and hustled him into the little run-down deli. The sour smell of lemon-scented ammonia and old cheese lay heavy in the air.

Chuck immediately went to turn around. "You have got to be kidding me. This place is crawling with germs and bacteria. There's no way I'm eating anything here."

"Sit!" Olivia demanded, then ordered two Cokes from the man behind the counter and brought them to the small table in the corner were Chuck had reluctantly pulled up a chair.

Olivia handed Chuck a Coke, but by now he looked ready to burst. "Evie, you have gone around the bend. That shock must've scrambled your brains. What has gotten into---"

"I'm not Evie." Olivia said tensely, leaning over the table and talking in a hushed whisper. "My name is Olivia Grace. I was born in 1899 and I was somehow zapped here into Evie's body while she was monitoring me on the Carpathia."

Olivia sat back, sorry that she had to drop the bombshell on him so suddenly, but feeling a sort of desperate panic now.

Chuck narrowed his eyes at her from across the table. "April Fool's Day is still three weeks away." he said carefully.

Olivia felt like reaching across the table and shaking him. "This is not a joke! Evie is still in this body, too, and neither of us likes this situation one bit. She said that she trusted you and that you might be able to get me back somehow."

"Time travel is impossible." Chuck said.

Olivia clenched her fists in frustration. "Seriously? You were able to get an actual film of the murder of Julius Caesar... and you want to tell me that *this* is impossible?"

"That's not the same." he said. "What we do can't affect or change things. We can look but not touch. It's the golden rule of applied quantum physics."

"And yet I'm here." Olivia almost shouted.

Chuck looked at her like she had truly lost her mind. "Listen, I get it. You recently suffered a serious electrical shock that disrupted you normal brain function. You're a mess. Don't worry about Dumas, I'll cover for you. You obviously still need some time to recover and…"

"I saw the wormhole that brought me here." Olivia interrupted.

Chuck actually laughed. "Ha! Now I know that you're nuts. That is scientifically impossible and you know it as well as I do."

"It was like a little dot, bobbing and weaving in the air." Olivia persisted. "It shimmered just like the St. Elmo's, but it was red instead of blue and it crackled and hissed. It touched me right on the forehead and the next thing I know, sparks are flying from Evie Deerbourne's computer and I am here."

Olivia was prepared to argue about this all day until Chuck finally believed her, but she stopped when she saw the queer expression come over Chuck's face. His eyebrows had creased and his mouth had turned down into a serious, thoughtful frown.

He was quiet for a long moment, then he looked at her again, a cloud of uncertainty on his face.

"It's…" he began, then frowned more. "That's…"

He looked at her for a long moment more with growing consternation. Something she had said had quieted his protests suddenly.

Finally, he leaned forward carefully. "Start from the beginning."

Chapter Eleven

By the third time Olivia recounted her story, Chuck had pulled out some paper and had begun jotting down an incomprehensible jumble of symbols and equations.

"It is the most improbable alignment of events imaginable." he murmured, looking over his notes and shaking his head. "It's as if a million variables all lined up at one precise instant to make something happen that should have been impossible."

Chuck looked up at Olivia and squinted at her eyes carefully, as if expecting to see something there. "So… you're actually sharing a body right now with Evie? Can she hear me? Can she talk?"

Olivia nodded. "She can hear and see everything that I can, but she can't talk. If I completely relax my hand, she can make it write a message."

Chuck's eyes widened in amazement. "So her consciousness must've receded to the left parietal lobe, which controls the movement for the right hand. That's just... I mean... wow. Can you... you know... feel her? Like her mind in there? Can you read her thoughts and she read yours?"

Olivia shook her head. "No. I had no idea she was in here until last night. I thought Natasha Cutiepeepers was writing me messages."

Chuck blinked at that, but decided not to pursue it.

"So, you know how this happened?" Olivia pressed. "Can it be undone?"

Chuck looked down at his notes and exhaled deeply. "This is all so radically new that I'm really just guessing here, but you said that you witnessed 'St. Elmos' right beforehand?"

Olivia nodded.

"Well," Chuck went on. "St. Elmo's Fire is a meteorological event that is actually electrically charged, luminous plasma that gathers and collects around grounded objects--- like ship's masts, for example. It usually happens in tandem with a thunderstorm and has been documented as far back as..."

Olivia felt her hand jump and pound impatiently on the table. She looked down at it wryly. "I think that Evie wants you to skip the history lesson and get to the point."

Chuck looked at her hand uncomfortably, then continued. "Right! Um... well. Let's make this simple, then. The St. Elmo's caused the wormhole to become electrically charged, too, which is why you could see it when you shouldn't have been able to. You weren't actually seeing the wormhole, but a point of charged plasma triggered by the signal that we were sending through."

"And that's why it cracked and hissed." Olivia said thoughtfully. "It was the electricity."

"Right. Now your brain is actually a complex collection of electrical impulses. Every thought, memory, desire, and dream held in your brain is a carefully crafted electro-chemical impulse. When the electrified wormhole touched your forehead, it acted as a conductor and the electrical

76

makeup of your brain rode the HistCorp data stream back through the wormhole and…"

"And zapped itself right into Evie." Olivia finished.

Chuck nodded. "Yes. Precisely. The surge also shorted out her workstation and gave her a jolt. That electrical shock rendered Evie unconscious, and since her brain activity was shut out in that instant, it became the perfect container for your mind to slip right in and fill… making you, Olivia Grace, the world's first time traveler."

"Lucky me." Olivia said impatiently. "Now how can you get me back?"

Chuck shook his head. "You're kidding, right?"

Olivia's chest tightened. "I thought that we've established that I am definitely not kidding."

Chuck waved his notes at her. "Did you not hear what I just said? This was a once in a billion years cosmic alignment. This was an act of God that brought you here. There is no way we can replicate that."

"I don't think that God wants me and Evie to be sharing a body for the rest of our lives."

Chuck shrugged. "Why would you even want to go back? You're gonna be a scientific superstar! Every quantum physicist in the world is going to want to meet you and…"

Olivia's hand involuntarily pounded on the table again, this time so hard that it nearly knocked over the two unopened cans of Coke.

Olivia looked down at her hand. "Evie doesn't like the sound of that and neither do I." she said.

She pulled Chuck's notes over to her side of the table and turned to a fresh page. She picked up his pencil and it had barely touched the paper before it started writing furiously.

we can try reverse modulation

Olivia had no idea what those words meant and showed the message to Chuck. He guffawed. "At what frequency, Evie? Would you suggest I just pick any random one? That would fry you both out for sure. We would only have one chance to broadcast."

"What are you talking about?" Olivia asked.

Chuck rolled his eyes as if trying to explain something that should have been readily obvious to a kindergartener. "The only reason your brain was transmitted whole and intact was that the electrical waves were moving at a precise frequency."

"Like the wireless set that Harold uses." Olivia said.

Chuck wrinkled his nose. "That's like saying that the cotton gin is sorta like a supercomputer, but yes... you get the idea."

"So if you tried to transmit my brain back at the wrong frequency, it would get all garbled and full of static. Instead of all of my nice, clear memories, I would end up as a zombie with a head full of messed up thoughts."

Chuck looked startled. "You've been watching too many movies kid."

Olivia shook her head. "Actually I've never seen a movie before. I just read a lot."

Chuck still eyed her doubtfully. "Right. Well, either way, kiddo, you wouldn't be a zombie—you would be dead. If it were even possible to recreate the circumstances that brought you here, we would only have one shot at this and unless we used the right frequency when we reversed it, then things would go terribly wrong for both you and Evie."

Olivia's hand was writing again.

I heard babies cry the message said.

Chuck looked bewildered. "What is that supposed to mean?"

Olivia's eyes widened. "That's right! I forgot about that. Evie must've heard it, too. Right as I passed through the wormhole."

"You heard babies crying?" Chuck asked doubtfully.

Olivia shook her head. "No. The wormhole said the words 'babies cry'."

Chuck's mouth dropped open. "Say huh?"

"Does that mean anything?" Olivia asked. "When Bubs and I first saw it, it said in a deep, gravelly voice 'How do you do?' I was so scared I almost passed out right there."

Chuck was looking at her again like she was crazy. "Wormholes... don't... talk." he said very slowly as if reconsidering whether or not Evie had lost her mind.

"This one did." Olivia said emphatically.

"That's imp---"

"Don't say that's impossible!" Olivia cut him off irritably.

Chuck threw up his hands. "But it is! You're telling me that this wormhole strolled up to you on the deck and, like a gentleman, tipped its hat and asked 'how do you do'?"

"It didn't have a hat." Olivia said through clenched teeth.

"And it didn't talk! It couldn't have!" Chuck nearly shouted.

i heard it too Olivia's hand scribbled.

"Oh, great." Chuck said sarcastically. "The crazy lady and her hand agree on something."

louis armstrong the pencil wrote suddenly.

They both looked down at the message. "Who?" they asked aloud in unison.

lyrics

louis armstrong.

Chuck let out an exasperated sigh, then pulled a device out of his pocket and started tapping it. A moment later, he frowned, looking down at the paper again. "She's right." he said. "They're part of the lyrics for a song by Louis Armstrong. *It's a Wonderful World*. But how is that..." Then an idea seemed to hit him and he started tapping on his device again, more purposely this time.

He looked at the tiny screen thoughtfully. "Radio. It was a radio frequency. The song was written long after your time, so it wasn't coming from your end—not that they even had

79

radio stations broadcasting music at that time." He mumbled, then looked up at her. "Here and now, though, in New York and the surrounding tri-state area, three radio stations were playing that song when you crossed over. Only one, though, was playing that exact lyric at the moment that Evie's computer fried. Eighty-eight point two—BHNS. Brooklyn's Heart and Soul."

Chuck's mouth twisted into an amused smile. "I think we've found your frequency."

Chapter Twelve

Between Evie's scribbled notes and Chuck's long-winded and rambling explanations, Olivia was able to build a vague impression of what they were planning to do.

That afternoon, Olivia found herself in the car with Chuck as he drove them out of the city and into the mountains, to the town of Jacob's Rest. Chuck's grandfather lived in a small farmhouse there and apparently Chuck wanted to retrieve some equipment that he had stored in his basement.

The drive was much calmer than her taxi ride had been, and Olivia found that upstate had not changed nearly as much in the last hundred years as the city had. Her family had come up to Tuxedo one weekend when she was seven, and the rolling green mountains looked every bit as beautiful now as they had back then.

Olivia found herself thinking about her father and she suddenly missed him so much that it was like a desperate ache in her chest.

"So tell me what you know about time travel." she said to Chuck as he drove, struggling to turn her thoughts from that painful ache.

He shrugged. "Like I said… it was never possible. You are the first one as far as anyone knows."

"But you must have some ideas. I read *The Time Machine* by HG Wells and he said that…""

Chuck waved his hand dismissively. "All pop culture nonsense. Marty McFly travelled through time in a Delorean. Bill and Ted used a phone booth. In *Somewhere in Time*, Christopher Reed went back in time by just closing his eyes and wishing really hard (to the year 1912, coincidentally). None of it has any scientific basis. In the television show *Quantum Leap*, Sam Beckett's consciousness jumped into other people's bodies, but it was all done with hocus-pocus and the other person wasn't still stuck inside with him. Unfortunately, this is real life and we're on our own figuring this one out."

"What happened to my body when I came here?" Olivia asked uneasily.

"Your guess is as good as mine." Chuck said. "Well, actually, I suppose my guess would probably be much better than yours in this case, but it would still be just a guess."

"Such as?" Olivia prompted.

"Well… there's the obvious. Without brain function, your body would just collapse and die."

Olivia cringed, hating to hear what she had feared all along.

"Of course," Chuck continued, "it's also possible that just your consciousness travelled here and enough of your basic brain functions remained to keep you breathing, your heart pumping, etc., in which case it would appear to most laymen that you were in a coma."

Olivia bit her lip and looked out at the trees passing by outside the car window. She worried more than ever about what her poor father must be thinking. Dead or coma--- either one would make him inconsolable.

"And there are some other... more interesting possibilities." Chuck considered.

Olivia turned to him. "What do you mean?"

"It's possible that when your consciousness travelled here, it was merely an electrical blueprint of your brain makeup, leaving the original intact. In that case, your original consciousness may have continued on."

Olivia frowned. "A... blueprint? You mean like... a copy? So there would be another Olivia that's still walking around on the decks of the Carpathia?"

"Yup." Chuck confirmed. "Completely unaware that her consciousness had been cloned and sent to the future. To her it may have been just a nasty shock and then life as normal."

Olivia didn't like the sound of that. "But she would be a copy of me."

"Er... actually she would be the original and you would just be an electrical imprint zapped into Evie. In that scenario, the easiest thing for us to do would be to just erase your consciousness from Evie's body so that she could have it back again. We wouldn't need to worry about sending you back through the wormhole because... well... you're already back there."

Olivia REALLY didn't like the sound of that. "But I am Olivia Grace! I'm here! I don't want to be erased!" she protested.

"It was just a guess." Chuck said defensively. "You told me to guess, so I'm just guessing out loud. I'm not saying that's the way it really is."

"Well, stop guessing! You're creeping me out."

Chuck raised his eyebrow. "Creeping you out? Did the kids say that in 1912?"

"No." Olivia said, still suppressing a shudder. "I must have read it."

Chuck suddenly slammed down on the brakes and the tires squealed as the car went shimmying off the road and onto the shoulder. He turned to her urgently. "What do you mean you *read it*? What have you been reading?"

Olivia looked at him, startled. "I went to the library yesterday and read up on some history. Why are we stopping?"

Chuck looked horrified. "What do you mean you read up on history? Why would you go and do something like that?"

Olivia was a little scared by the sudden intensity of Chuck's glare. She swallowed. "I travelled through time a hundred and fifteen years into the future. I read some books to catch up on things. What's the big deal?"

Chuck's face had gone white as he stared at her, almost speechless. Olivia's hand twitched in her lap and she looked down to see her fingers grasping for a pencil that was in the cup holder.

Olivia retrieved the pencil and put a pad of paper in her lap. Immediately, Evie began to write.

quantum theory states that–

Chuck looked down at the message that was being scratched across the paper and he looked annoyed. "Oh, stop, Evie! Don't you quote quantum theory to me. Did you know about this?"

yes but–

Chuck threw up his hands in frustration and turned irritably to watch the traffic passing by. "You are really asking for a huge leap of faith here." he mumbled.

Olivia was exasperated. "Would one of you mind telling me what the problem is? Why does it matter that I read about history?"

chuck is worried about a paradox Evie wrote.

Chuck glanced down at the pad and shook his head. "It will take too long to write it. Just let me tell her." he sighed. Then, he leveled a serious gaze at Olivia. "I'm worried about a paradox." he said frankly.

Olivia looked at her paper, then back up at him expectantly. "Um... you're gonna have to give me more than that."

Chuck sighed again as if he couldn't believe he had to explain something so simple and obvious.

"You travelling forward in time is no problem." he began.

Olivia snorted. "I beg your pardon! It's a big problem for *me*!"

Chuck rolled his eyes. "No, I mean big-picture wise. There's no chance of you disrupting the time-space continuum. You could travel ahead in time, adjust and blend in, and live your life in the future without consequences. We all travel forward in time naturally anyway at a rate of one minute per minute. It's the normal way of things."

Chuck then leveled a serious look at her. "The problems come if someone tries to travel the other way."

"You said that nobody has ever time-travelled before." Olivia reminded him.

"Right. And that's the problem. Nobody knows for sure what would happen, but there are two main schools of thought. The classical, Einsteinian, pre-quantum thinking says that backwards travel must be impossible because of the likelihood of a paradox."

Olivia threw up her hands. "Still don't know what that word means."

"Well, there's the classic example of the grandmother paradox. What if you went back in time and met your own maternal grandmother before your own mother was born?"

"That would be wonderful!" Olivia smiled at the thought.

"... and killed her?" Chuck finished.

Olivia looked horrified. "Why on earth would I kill my own grandmother!?"

Chuck pushed on. "I'm not saying that you would. Let's say it was an accident... but it's something that would not have happened if you had not travelled back in time."

"That's terrible!" Olivia gasped.

Chuck rolled his eyes. "You're missing the point here. It's just... think about what that would mean for a moment. If you killed your own grandmother before she could have kids, then your own mother could never be born and if your mother never existed then you could never be born yourself, right?"

Olivia paled. "Yikes! So..." Olivia considered this for a moment. "So... what would happen? You would just disappear?"

"Nobody knows." Chuck said. "But that's not the paradox. The paradox is this: if you were never actually born, then you never existed to go back in time. If you never went back in time, then your grandmother *wouldn't* be killed."

Olivia tried to wrap her head around that. "So... then you *would* be born, right?"

"But if you were born, then you would kill your grandmother." Chuck said.

"Then you wouldn't be born? Wait... which is it?"

Chuck smiled. "That's it. That's why it's a paradox. There is no answer. It seems like an impossible situation... an endless loop. That's why Einstein declared that backwards time travel is impossible. He said that the universe or God or whoever is watching out for things just wouldn't let it happen. Other people thought that if a paradox could happen, it would tear the fabric of time to bits and destroy everything in existence."

Olivia looked shaken and swallowed uneasily. "But... I'm not going back to meet my own grandmother, so no chance for a paradox here, right?"

Chuck pushed up his glasses. "Oh, that was just a simple example. The fact is if you had just come here and gone back without learning anything at all about your own future, then we might be okay. But now if you go back and change something, then you could change the entire course of history."

"But that's still in my future. How will that cause a paradox?" Olivia asked.

"Let's say you came forward in time, learned about something that was going to happen, and decided you wanted to change it." Chuck began, and Olivia remembered the images of the Titanic survivors arriving on the Carpathia, looking lost and terrified. Olivia's hand twitched slightly, but Chuck continued without noticing. "So you change history and through the twists and turns of fate, HistCorp never comes into existence. Now if HistCorp doesn't exist, then you can't be pulled forward in time…"

Olivia understood. "And if I never go forward in time, then I never changed history, so it becomes a paradox…"

"Exactly." Chuck finished.

Olivia's hand was reaching for the pencil again, but she covered it with her other hand and bit her lip thoughtfully. "So when we started, you said that there were two schools of thought. What is the other?"

"Quantum physics" Chuck said. "It says that there are an infinite number of timelines existing side by side and everything that COULD happen has happened in one of those timelines somewhere. There's a timeline where dinosaurs evolved instead of mammals and reptiles are driving cars. There's a timeline where Germany won World War Two. There's a timeline where the world is still controlled by a modern Roman Empire that never collapsed. All of it is true."

Chuck licked his lips thoughtfully. "In quantum time-travel theory, paradoxes aren't a problem. If you went back in time and killed your own grandmother, then she would be dead and you would have jumped over onto a timeline where you, in fact, were never born. No problem at all. The original timeline still exists, where she is still alive and you were born, but because of your actions, you are now on a different timeline where history will unfold differently. The time traveler isn't changing history, they are moving themselves to different timelines."

Olivia looked a little less apprehensive. "Well that sounds… better. Is that the way it is?"

Chuck nodded slowly. "We think so. Everything we've done at HistCorp and all of the advances in physics for decades have been based on quantum theory. That is almost definitely the way things are."

"Almost definitely?" Olivia repeated.

"Right." Chuck nodded, his eyebrows furrowed in thought. "Except..." he trailed off uncertainly.

Olivia didn't like that pause. "Except what?"

There was a scratching noise and Olivia realized that her hand had freed itself and started writing again.

except none of the wormholes show us dinosaurs driving cars

Chuck looked down at the note and snorted. "Right. If wormholes can truly come out anywhere, then some of them should show us some of these other timelines. Every one we've ever looked through only shows us our own, though. It's been the big stumbling block in every quantum theory since this has all started. Either the wormholes are limited to just moving within a single timeline or..."

"Or there is only one timeline." Olivia finished. "Which means that if I do go back and change something... even accidentally..."

"You could destroy the entire universe." Chuck said matter-of-factly.

"I see." Olivia said, feeling a pit in her stomach. Now she understood why Chuck had slammed on the brakes and stopped the car so suddenly.

He surprised her, though, by looking at her for a long moment and then finally giving a resigned shrug. "Ah, well." he said, putting the car back into gear. "What the heck. Let's do it anyway."

Chapter Thirteen

The basement of Chuck's grandfather's house was piled high with an extraordinary menagerie of old machines, electrical equipment, and odd-looking tools. When Olivia first saw it, she told Chuck that it was exactly how she imagined the laboratory of Dr. Frankenstein to look, and Chuck seemed to take that as an immense compliment.

"I grew up here." he said, digging through a big pile of wires and spare parts near the back. "This was sort of my laboratory in a way. If I hadn't become a quantum physicist, I would have loved to be an inventor." He grinned at Olivia and in that moment he looked strikingly like Bubs—a little kids full of wild ideas.

Olivia fingered the crank of what she recognized immediately as a dusty old Victrola music player. She looked at it in amazement. "My neighbor got one of these just before my mom died." Olivia said, running her finger through the blanket of dust. "Mrs. Peabody…" Olivia smiled, to herself, lost in a distant memory. "She only had one disc and she would invite everyone in to listen to the music it made. We were all so amazed. It seemed impossible that music could be captured on a disc and played back. We thought that such an amazing device must surely be the most clever thing that would ever be invented."

Chuck glanced up. "Yup. That's a Victor Victrola model XI, released in 1910. Could you imagine how freaked your neighbor would have been if she had seen what an iPod could do?"

He grunted as he lifted a heavy box from the pile he had been digging through. "Bingo!" he said. "Found it."

Olivia looked at the box he was lifting. It was covered with dials and knobs of all sizes and looked like it had more dust on it than the Victrola. "What did you find, exactly?"

"Radio transmitter." Chuck said. "I used to broadcast my own station with this baby. Radio CHK. It was only strong enough to transmit 100 feet or so, but I would setup behind the bushes on the side of the road and for a few glorious seconds, passing cars could pick up the sweet sounds of Chuck." He looked at the old box with a nostalgic gleam in his eye.

"Sounds... special." Olivia said carefully.

"Oh, it was! Now I just need to modify this puppy to plug into the HistCorp network so we can send your brain back on the right frequency."

"Eighty-eight point two." Olivia said.

"The heart and soul of Brooklyn." Chuck echoed, diving back into the piles of parts in search for something else.

Olivia picked up a box with the words "Pet Rock" across the top. Curiously, she opened the lid and inside found an ordinary-looking rock rattling around inside an otherwise empty box. Experimentally, she poked the rock, expecting it to move or make a sound or do anything at all pet-like. Inexplicably, though, it seemed to be just a rock.

Olivia closed the lid and set the rock back down again, trying to control her impatience as Chuck rummaged through his old junk. She couldn't help but think about her father, mourning her, thinking that she was gone forever. The sooner she could get back to him, the better. (Also, Olivia couldn't help but secretly consider that she had been here three days. She had left on April 11, 1912 and the Titanic would hit the iceberg on the night of the 14th. She knew that all of the talk about paradoxes and changing history meant that she absolutely could NOT prevent it, but a little clock in her head still ticked away the hours towards that impending event...)

Then, a terrible idea hit her. "If I've been dead for three days back in 1911, won't my body be decomposing when I'm put back into it?"

Chuck didn't even look up from the box of wires he was rifling through. "Nah. The cycle time on the Carpathia feed was super low, right Evie? What was it again?"

Olivia's hand wrote in the dust across the surface of the Victrola.

.0081

Olivia read the numbers aloud to Chuck.

Chuck nodded. "Yup. See. Told ya. No worries."

"Hello." Olivia called. "Twelve year old girl here. I have no idea what a 'cycle time' is or why it should put my mind at ease."

Chuck sighed again, pausing in his digging. "Do you remember how you said the wormhole moved back and forth when you saw it?"

Olivia nodded. "Yes. It seemed to be flying about like a lightning bug."

"Well... all of them do that. They dip and dive and float all around... drifting in the ether and buffered by cosmic winds. Watching some of the feeds for too long will really make you seasick, honestly."

Olivia rolled her fingers impatiently. "Still not hearing the point here."

Chuck hurried on. "Right, well, not only do they move about in space, they also are moving through time... and all of them move at a different speed, which we call the cycle time. Some of them we look through and things seem to be going by in a blur because that wormhole is moving through time slowly at that end and the world is moving on at a normal speed around it. In some of them, things seem to be moving in slow motion because that end of the wormhole is speeding by faster than the normal pace, The computers fix the feeds so they look normal when we play them back, but hardly any of them actually pass by at the normal speed. You remember that Lincoln assassination clip they played in the informational video? That took seventeen months to film five minutes. When you looked at the raw feed, it looked like it was just standing still. The computer sped it up to make it watchable."

Olivia covered her eyes. "My brain is going to explode. Make it super simple."

Chuck scratched his chin thoughtfully. "Alright. Um... let's see. A cycle time of .0081 means that the Carpathia feed is moving ahead at about sixty-seven seconds a day."

Olivia blinked at that. "So, I've only been gone..."

Chuck went back to his rummaging. "About three and a half minutes so far. Your body is not decomposing."

Olivia exhaled a deep breath of relief. "My father probably doesn't even know what's happened, either."

Chuck shook his head. "Nope. Probably not. Of course, we really should get you back tonight."

Olivia agreed. "Yes, I know we'll all be happy when this is over."

"Not only that." Chuck said, carefully pulling open the back of his transmitter and blowing out the dust. "If your body really is lying there not breathing, then anything past four minutes and you're going to have irreversible brain damage."

"What do you mean 'brain damage'?" she asked urgently.

Chuck sighed. "Really? I have to explain that one? I thought that it was pretty self-explanatory. See, your brain needs oxygen or else it..."

"I understand that part, I just wish I had known about this sooner!" Olivia sputtered.

Chuck made some final adjustments before closing the box he was working on. "How would that have helped?" he asked. "You would have just panicked."

"Well, I'm panicking now! How much time... exactly... do we have?"

Chuck glanced at his watch. "Er... well... we should probably try to get you back before 10:32 tonight... or somewhere thereabouts."

Olivia looked at an old clock that hung above a cluttered workbench in the nearby shadows. It was 2:30 in the afternoon.

She bit her lip nervously. "What else do you think we'll need to..."

Before she could finish, though, there was a crash of glass from across the basement. Chuck and Olivia both turned in time to see that some kind of canister had broken through the window and was now rolling to a stop by Olivia's feet.

They stared at it in bewilderment. To Olivia, it looked like a silver soup can.

Chuck looked baffled. "What in the world is..."

Then there was a muffled "pop!" and a thick cloud of white smoke began erupting from the canister. Even as it did, there was a clatter as two more of the silver canisters flew through the window and rolled across the floor.

""It's gas!" Chuck yelled out suddenly, and in that moment the first fumes hit Olivia and a searing pain tore through her mouth and nose. Her eyes began to sting painfully.

Blinded and gagging, Olivia quickly became disoriented as the basement filled with a choking cloud of gas. She heard a crash of splintering wood- as if someone were tearing a door down, then the voices of men all around, barking orders at each other.

A hand grabbed her roughly and Olivia cried out and tried to pull free. In the next moment, a hand clamped over her mouth and she heard Chuck's voice in her ear. "Get low. Stay with me."

Olivia blindly latched on and let Chuck lead her through the burning fumes while the heavy sound of boots and men knocking over piles of junk crashed all around them. Olivia cringed as some of the searching men passed nearly on top of them, but Chuck guided them to a place near the base of the back wall where he pulled aside a piece of plywood and revealed a hollowed out hole in the cinderblock wall and the dirt beyond.

He pulled Olivia into the crevasse and slid the wood back into place.

The air in here was cleaner and free of fumes. Eventually, Olivia began to breathe normally again, although the tears still poured from her stinging eyes and her throat felt like it was on fire. Chuck was huddled beside her in the darkness of the hollow dugout and Olivia could hear him struggling to muffle his own choked breathing.

They listened as the men who had stormed the basement continued to crash around, overturning tables and piles of stacked boxes in their search. Finally, they heard a man stop close outside the plywood wall of their hideout. There was a burst of static as he spoke into a radio. "Team Alpha to Home. We're at the extraction point but the subjects have not been secured. Repeat--- the subjects are not secured."

The voice of a woman broke through the static to respond irritably. "You let them get away?"

"We have the place surrounded. We're not sure how they were able to escape our perimeter."

The woman scoffed. "You're an idiot. Get your team back here and regroup."

"Yes, 'mam. Copy that." The man's voice said, cutting off the radio. "I hate that woman." He mumbled to himself, then Olivia jumped as he raised his voice to rally his men.

"We're moving out!" he yelled, and there was a flurry of heavy boots and shouted orders as the men cleared out of the basement.

In a few minutes time, the only sound remaining was the hushed breathing of Olivia and Chuck echoing hollowly in the hidden alcove. She wiped her burning eyes and strained to hear any other sounds through the wooden wall.

It was nearly five minutes later when Olivia whispered breathlessly in the darkness. "Who was that?"

Chuck's voice was hoarse and cracked when he responded. "They must be Section 18." he choked. She saw now that he had the radio transmitter pulled up against his chest and was clutching it tightly.

"Who?" Olivia asked.

"They're from HistCorp." he rasped, swallowing to try to ease his burning throat. "I think that things just got much, much more complicated."

Chapter Fourteen

Back in the car again, Chuck nervously checked his rearview mirror every few seconds and constantly craned his head up to look at the sky through the windshield as if he expected more Section 18 commandos to drop down on them from the clouds at any moment.

His face was white and his bloodshot eyes were wild and nervous. Olivia clutched the car door as he swerved wildly around another turn.

"Chuck, calm down or you're going to get us killed."

"Me?" he nearly choked. "No, you're the one who's going to get us killed. Those guys were after you."

"After me? Why? What do they want with me?"

Chuck took another turn so fast that Olivia was tossed roughly against her door. "You're kidding right? Hmm... let me see... why would they be after you? Oh! Hey! Here's a thought! Maybe because you're a freakin' TIME TRAVELLER! You've done what they've been trying to figure out how to do for centuries... and they probably want to pick you apart to find out how you did it."

"But... how would they even know?" Olivia gasped. "You're the only one I've told."

Chuck gritted his teeth and cut another look behind them. "This is Section 18 we're talking about here. They know EVERYTHING."

"Why?" Olivia asked, nervously checking in her own rearview mirror. "What is Section 18?"

Chuck laughed. "Oh, come on! You didn't buy that whole informational video did you? The one with Dumas standing there smiling and telling the world that what they do at HistCorp is all about learning the truth about our past for a better tomorrow? Sure, some of that stuff is true, but there's no profit in educating the world about history. That's not what HistCorp is really all about."

Olivia was flustered. "I don't get it."

"Wormholes come out anywhere, right? You heard that in the video. Out of several trillions, we're lucky if even one shows anything recognizable... much less historically significant."

"Right." Olivia said carefully. "I got that part. There are lots and lots of them and most of them go nowhere."

"Right. Even when the computers find one that might have something, it takes a human analyst like Evie or I to decide if it's anything important. Sections one through ten at HistCorp are all assigned to monitoring wormholes in specific time periods. Evie and I are in section nine, which monitors basically the last two hundred years."

"Go on." Olivia said.

"Well, there are also sections eleven through seventeen, which monitor wormholes that come out in a time *ahead* of ours."

Olivia furrowed her eyebrows in confusion. "The future? They can see the future?"

Chuck shook his head. "No. Not really… but that doesn't stop them from trying. The feeds we get from the future wormholes are just an incomprehensible blur of constantly changing images. The further away in the future it is, the more random and indecipherable it gets. They work the computers constantly, trying to create programs and algorithms that could make sense of things, but the fact is that they can't see the future because the future… from our point of view… is not set yet."

"Alright." Olivia nodded. "So what about Section 18? What do they do that they need their own private army?"

Chuck's mouth twisted into a sour expression. "Section 18 is HistCorp' best kept secret. Those guys look through wormholes that come out in our own present. Sometimes, they're looking at things that happened just a few minutes before, but the fact is that they can potentially look *anywhere* in the world without anyone knowing that they are watching."

Olivia looked at him sharply. "They're spies? That's what this is all about?"

Chuck nodded. "Heck yeah, that's what this is all about. When all of this started years ago, Dumas used the wormholes to find a terrorist that the government had been hunting for decades. He was tucked away in some cave on the other side of the world, but one of the feeds picked him up. Once the government found out what HistCorp could do, Dumas got real rich real fast. Now they have computers looking through wormholes all over the world, keeping track of everything that's going on. HistCorp has about five hundred people like Evie and I sorting through historical feeds to keep the public happy. Section 18 has over five *thousand* people sorting through feeds around the clock."

Olivia was stunned. "So that's how they knew. They were watching us."

Chuck nodded. "They're always watching us. The only way to avoid them is to just keep moving."

With that, Chuck took another turn that brought them onto a larger four-lane road.

Olivia struggled to remain calm in light of this startling new development. "But what can we do now? If we try to go back to the HistCorp building, then they'll have us." Her right hand started to quiver and Olivia snatched up a pencil and a pad.

remote connection?

Olivia read the message to Chuck and he winced. "I don't know about that, Evie. I could probably get to the feed, but then you're talking about sending Olivia's brain over a long distance and hoping the signal doesn't get scrambled along the way." He chewed his fingernail thoughtfully as he drove. "Still, it might work. We need one more thing, though, before we can..."

Chuck was interrupted by a burst of classical music from his pocket. It was Beethoven's 5th Symphony. He fumbled at it for a moment, swerving dangerously off the edge of the road, and then pulled out his cell phone. When he looked at the screen he nearly choked. Casting an uneasy glance at Olivia, he hesitated, then flipped open the phone and cleared his throat. "Hello?" he asked shakily.

There was a tense moment of silence, then he looked at Olivia. Carefully, he pulled the phone from his ear and offered it to her. "It's for you." he said.

Olivia looked at the phone in surprise. "For Evie?" she mouthed.

Chuck shook his head. "No. It's for you, Olivia."

Stunned, Olivia reached out and picked up the phone with a trembling hand. She put it to her ear and spoke in a choked whisper. "Hello?"

"Hello, Miss Grace." the woman on the other end said smoothly. "I trust you are well. Unharmed?"

Olivia cast a terrified look at Chuck, who was watching her with wide eyes.

"I'm... fine." Olivia said carefully.

"I'm glad to hear it." the woman said. "I take it that by now you know who I am?"

Olivia swallowed. "I'm assuming that I'm talking to Minerva Dumas."

"Very good. Your... situation... has caused quite a stir of curiosity around here. I am so very anxious to meet you, dear."

Olivia almost guffawed. "I can tell by the way your men came after us."

The woman continued without pause. "Idiot soldier boys. They think that the solution to everything is storming in and tearing things apart. No tact at all."

"I was under the impression that you had sent them." Olivia said.

"They got a little ahead of themselves." the woman soothed. "They were my backup plan. I had sincerely hoped to have this discussion with you first so we could talk woman to woman and work things out sensibly."

Olivia twisted her mouth. "Well it didn't work out that way, did it?"

"Regrettably, no." Dumas said. "However, I do hope that you will still consider coming to see me on your own terms. You have so much to offer us."

"And yet you have nothing to offer me." Olivia said.

"We will send you back to your father." Dumas suggested.

"No you won't"

The woman laughed lightly. "Fine. You have me there. Your body would be long dead by the time we are finished studying you. You're actually quite sharp for a twelve-year-old little girl."

"So I've been told." Olivia said coolly.

Dumas sighed. "I can see that we're going to have to do this the hard way, aren't we dearie?"

"I suppose we are."

"Regrettable."

"It is." Olivia agreed.

"Well alright. Please tell Mr. Ferryman to drive safely. I'll be seeing you both soon."

"Don't be so sure." Olivia said evenly.

There was a click and the line went dead. Chuck was watching Olivia with wide eyes as she handed him his phone back.

"I think we've made her mad now." Olivia told him.

Chuck flinched. "I can't believe I let you and Evie talk me into this." he said anxiously. Then, he took his cell phone, rolled down his window, and tossed it out.

Chapter Fifteen

The sun was setting when Chuck pulled into the parking lot of Arden Hill Hospital.

They were still upstate, and the twilight sky over the mountains around them helped to soothe Olivia's shaken and uneasy thoughts. Chuck sat silently behind the wheel of the idling car, intently watching the entrance to the Emergency Room.

"What exactly are we waiting for?" Olivia asked.

"The last piece of the puzzle." he said.

Olivia sighed, frustrated that he wouldn't tell her more. She looked up at the darkening sky and the stars winking on above. When she looked up at them, a thought suddenly occurred to Olivia.

"Have you found any aliens?" Olivia asked.

This made Chuck turn to her. "Say what?"

"Aliens." Olivia said. "If the wormholes come out anywhere, then some of them must come out on other planets in other galaxies."

"We're limited by the 4.5B rule." he replied.

When he saw Olivia's confusion, he sighed and turned his attention back to watching the Emergency Room entrance. "You explain it to her, Evie."

Olivia's hand began to write.

the wormholes that we can observe all have a 4.5 billion time and space limit. none of them look back in time further than 4.5 billion years and none of them come out in space more than 4.5 billion miles away. we think that there might be another type of wormhole... bigger maybe... that we haven't been able to find yet, but all of the ones that we can work with are limited by this rule.

"Weird." Olivia muttered.

"It drives them crazy." Chuck said without turning back to her. "They can't see back to how the Earth was first formed and they can't see anything beyond our own solar system. Some people call it 'The God Rule' because they think that it's God's way of keeping His secrets and saying that some things are just none of our business."

Olivia smiled. "I like that idea."

Chuck snorted, but didn't say anything else. A moment later, the twilit parking lot was splashed with flashing lights and an ambulance pulled up to the Emergency Room entrance. Chuck leaned forward and unlatched his seatbelt. "Alright. Here we go."

The ambulance parked and the medics opened up the back and pulled out a patient on a stretcher. As they set him up on a gurney and wheeled him inside, Chuck opened his door and slipped out, running across the parking lot. Olivia watched him as he crept up to the back of the open ambulance and rummaged around inside for a moment.

The pencil in her hand scratched across the paper.

what is he doing?

103

Olivia shook her head. "I have no idea."

A moment later, Chuck dashed back across the parking lot towards the car, carrying a white case with blue lettering across it. He pulled open his door and tossed it into the backseat.

"Alright!" he said. "I think we have everything that we need. Now, let's see if we can find a quiet spot someplace and send you back in time."

They ended up in a place called "Smith's Clove Park" in the tiny town of Monroe, New York. It was 9:45 when they stopped and Olivia was watching the minutes tick by quickly, trying not to imagine her body lying lifeless on the deck of the Carpathia. They had forty-five minutes to get her back.

Chuck drove off of the road and right into a grassy field, stopping at the crest of a small hill. It was completely dark now and the stars glistened high up in the sky. It wasn't as clear and beautiful as it would have been huddled in the crow's nest at midnight in the middle of the Atlantic, but Olivia found it beautiful just the same. She marveled at how the world had changed so much in the last hundred years, but the stars remained as unchanged and beautiful as ever.

Chuck turned off his headlights, but left the motor running so he could plug in his equipment. Before he got out, though, he sat in the idling car, staring through the darkened windshield, and he took a deep breath, as if preparing himself to go into battle.

"Are you ready?" he asked.

Olivia nodded firmly. "Ready." she said, and when she looked down a moment later, she saw that her hand had written the same.

It was 10:22.

Although the park was empty, Olivia and Chuck would jump and look about warily at the smallest sounds they heard. It was unnerving work, and the clock counting down the minutes to Olivia's certain death only made things worse.

"Ten minutes until I get brain damage, Chuck!" she warned tensely. "I really, really don't want to have brain damage, Chuck!"

Chuck nodded quickly as he adjusted the dials on the transmitter he'd brought. "I know, I know. Almost set." He carefully set the transmitter to precisely 88.2, then looked up at her and grinned. "88 miles per hour! When this baby hits 88, you're going to see some serious stuff!" He laughed and looked at her expectantly.

Olivia frowned at him. "88 miles per hour? What are you talking about? We're not getting back in the car, are we?"

Chuck looked disappointed. "*Back to the Future*! Doc Brown! Classic time travel movie. C'mon!"

Olivia narrowed her eyes at him. "I will be dead if we don't send me back in nine minutes. I'm *not* in the mood for jokes right now."

Chuck turned to the laptop he'd setup and started typing. "Women just don't have a sense of humor..." he muttered. After a moment, he nodded. "Yup. Just as I thought. They locked us out of the HistCorp network. All of my access codes have been revoked"

Olivia's eyes widened. "What does that mean?"

Chuck smiled. "It means that I get to break in the fun way!" He started typing with determination. "C'mon, guys. Really? You really thought you could keep out Chuck Ferryman? Buncha wannabe cyber-sissies. You guys have no idea who you're... dealing with." He pressed a final button, then grinned up at her. "Alright. I'm in."

Olivia looked at the screen of his computer and saw a hazy grey image that didn't seem to be moving at all. "Are you sure that's it?"

Chuck nodded. "Remember the cycle time difference. One second there takes about twenty-two minutes here. This is the unbuffered feed. It's just gonna look like a still picture."

Olivia squinted at the hazy grey picture and after a moment, she could make out the shape of the ship's railing, the lifeboat crane, and...

She let out a gasp. "That's me!"

Chuck, who was opening up the white case he had snatched from the ambulance, glanced up at the screen. "Yup."

Olivia swallowed. "I look dead!"

Chuck nodded. "You are, but we're going to see if we can do something about that." He pulled some silver and white paddles from the white case and started flipping some switches.

"What are those?" Olivia asked suspiciously.

"Defibrillator." he said, "They're supposed to kick-start a person's heart when it stops, but we're gonna use them to simulate the power spike that sent you here."

Olivia became aware of a distant thrumming sound and looked up. Several miles away, a bright light was skimming towards them over the tree line. "Um, Chuck... is that..."

He frowned at the approaching light. "If we're gonna do this, it's going to have to be now." he said.

He switched on the old transmitter and the lights flickered on dimly. He plugged a cable from the transmitter into his laptop, then plugged in another cable and gave it a strong pull until it snapped in half. He took the frayed wires and taped them to Olivia's forehead.

"Sorry we don't have time to do this any better." he said.

"If it works, then I forgive you." she answered nervously, watching the light as it got nearer. It was a helicopter, flying at them low and fast. It would be here in less than a minute.

Chuck set one of the defibrillator paddles into Olivia's palm and closed her hand around it. "Hold on to this." he said, then placed the other paddle on the top surface of the transmitter.

Olivia swallowed nervously. "Listen, Chuck. In case I don't... you know... I just... I wanted to thank you and Evie for your help."

Chuck smiled at her. "This was the adventure I've been waiting my whole life for." he said. "Thank *you* Olivia."

Olivia forced a smile and took a steadying breath. "I'm ready." she said. The thumping of the helicopter was so loud now that it shook the ground and vibrated in her chest.

Chuck pressed some buttons on the laptop, then readied his hand on the defibrillator switch. "Here we go then. Five, four, three..."

"Wait!" Olivia called over the tremor of the helicopter. She pointed at the radio transmitter, which had gone dark.

Chuck looked at it and thumped it hard on top, making it light up again. "Sorry." he said sheepishly. "Loose wire. Alright. Here we go..."

There was suddenly a crack from the sky, followed by two more, and Olivia felt something pull at her shoulder. She looked down and was bewildered to see a hole in her shirt there. A moment later, a dark stain began to spread from the hole and she felt something warm and wet spreading against her skin.

Chuck looked at the strange hole in confusion. "Have you... have you just been shot?"

Then Olivia looked down at two rapidly growing dark stains in Chuck's own shirt. One on his arm and one near his stomach.

He looked at her horrified expression, then followed her gaze down to his own shirt. "Hey, look... I think I've been shot, too." he said curiously, reaching out to touch one of the tattered holes. He looked up at her with a shaky grin. "Wow. I really didn't expect that to happen."

107

Then his eyes rolled up and he collapsed sideways.

The bright light from the helicopter played across the ground and a strong wind kicked up clouds of dirt around them now. The sound was almost deafening. Olivia began to feel light-headed as more blood soaked her shirt. She looked at the screen of the laptop and the hazy image of herself lying on the deck of the Carpathia a hundred years ago. She thought it was so strange that she was dying there and here at the same time, in two different places a hundred years apart. She collapsed onto her back, squinting up into the torrent of dust and wind as the helicopter circled above her for a place to land.

Just before she lost consciousness, she found herself overwhelmed with a desperate sadness… not for herself, but for her father who would now be all alone in the world.

Evie's body lay still and unmoving for a long moment, the blood from her wound now spilling quickly onto the dark grass. On the nearby computer screen, Olivia's body lay in nearly the same position. The circling helicopter finally landed and before it even touched the ground, men in heavy boots were storming from its open doors.

As they rushed to surround the two bodies on the grass, Evie's hand twitched.

At first, it seemed like nothing more than the trembling spasms of a dying woman, but then her hand began to slowly grope and pull its way towards the nearby defibrillator. When her fingers found the buttons and switches there, they felt across them weakly until they found the one they were looking for.

The arriving soldiers, in the commotion of the wind and light and dust, saw too late what was happening.

As the last bit of strength seeped from her fingertips, Evie Deerbourne... the real Evie Deerbourne... made one final desperate attempt to save the little girl that had unexpectedly become a part of her life.

Her hand threw the switch.

Chapter Sixteen

Olivia jolted awake, her muscles flailing and clenched as if an electric shock coursed through her body, setting every limb on fire.

She gulped and gasped for breath like a drowning victim who had just broken the surface at the last possible instant. White spots popped like fireworks behind her eyes and the torrent of wind around her was like a banshee scream assaulting her ears. She writhed and struggled like this for a long moment as uncontrollable seizures wracked her body, and through it all she felt the terrible uneven pounding of her heart as it fought to find its rhythm again.

Eventually, the tremors stopped and she was sitting up, trembling and breathing hard... trying to blink away her blindness to see where she was. Hazy and indistinct silhouettes slowly became visible in the darkness: a metal railing, a stowed lifeboat and crane... then she felt the gentle rolling sway of the Carpathia beneath her and a surge of hope swelled up in her chest.

The cool, salty night air filled her lungs as the spots before her eyes slowly cleared. Her heart pounded furiously in her chest, and she still shook with the aftershocks of her seizure.

The last thing that she remembered was Chuck collapsing. A lump rose in her throat at the shocking thought that he had given his life to save her. And then there was Evie… what had happened to her? She had barely known them, yet they had sacrificed so much for her.

The St. Elmo's was gone, and so was any sign of the wormhole that had caused all of this in the first place. It was just Olivia, sitting on the wooden deck as if she had collapsed there moments before and had never actually gone anywhere. As the familiar feel of her home settled back into place around her, the first nagging doubts already began to creep into her head.

I was surely dreaming. Olivia thought. *Maybe I was shocked by the St. Elmo's. Bubs said it was harmless, but he's just a child… what does he know? Somehow, it shocked me and I collapsed on the deck for a few seconds… having a very strange and realistic dream…*

Olivia started to move and found that her muscles were aching and sore. Most disturbing of all, she found that her right hand would not move. She lifted it and prodded it with her other hand, but she couldn't feel anything. She concentrated hard on making the fingers move, but they remained limp and unmoving despite her most concerted efforts.

As Olivia was trying to rub some feeling back into it, she was startled by a voice behind her.

"Olivia? Are you all right?"

She spun to see Bubs there in his oversized shirt, looking around the darkened deck warily. "Where's the ghost?" he asked timidly. "Is it gone?"

Instead of answering, Olivia lunged forward and hugged Bubs tightly, nearly overwhelmed by the conflicting emotions that swelled within her. Bubs instantly struggled to pull free and when he was able to stumble back away from her a few steps, he choked and sputtered. "Jeez, Olivia! What's gotten into you?"

"I'm back." Olivia said as tears rolled down her cheeks. "It worked. I'm really back."

"What are you talking about?" Bubs stammered in exasperation. "You didn't go anywhere!"

But Olivia was sure that she had. She rubbed her dead hand worriedly and pulled herself up from the deck. It was a strange sensation to be six inches shorter again. With Bubs watching her, she reached up and pulled a lock of her hair into view. She twisted her mouth into a grin and showed it to him. "Red hair." she said.

Bubs just looked at her like she had lost her mind.

Olivia felt the overwhelming urge to run down to the bottom of the ship and jump into her father's arms. The Carpathia was cutting through the waves at a brisk speed, though, and she knew that he was down there furiously shoveling coal to keep them going. She would have to wait until his shift was over in the morning.

She climbed through the tangle of pipes back into her hidden cubbyhole near the wireless room. Next door, Harold was still hunched over his set and furiously tapping out messages to the mainland before they got too far out at sea for the signal to reach. Even in her hidden room, she could hear his rhythmic tapping through the wall that separated them.

Olivia slid up in front of her tiny, clouded mirror and squinted at her reflection there. She ran her good hand over her face... her familiar green eyes... her freckled and spotted nose. "Hello Olivia" she said to herself, and relished the sound of her own voice coming from her lips.

She pulled at her unruly hair and sighed. "I'm glad to be back." she muttered. "But I will miss your beautiful hair, Evie."

She closed her eyes and tried again to shake away the terrible image of Chuck's shocked expression in that moment when he had realized that he had been shot. She tried to forget the feeling of lying in Evie's body, bleeding in the grass.

Maybe they're still alive. She thought to herself... but she knew this was an empty hope. She knew what had really happened. She had felt Evie's body dying.

Olivia shuddered as the ship rolled over a swell and tilted slightly to starboard. She blinked again at her cloudy reflection and thought about the other thing that had been looming like a black cloud in her mind.

It was still April 11.

Somewhere on the other side of the world, the Titanic would soon be steaming towards them with over two thousand people onboard. She closed her eyes and tried to block out the memory of all the terrible pictures she had seen that day in the library.

Before the Carpathia had set sail from New York, the world had been abuzz with news of the grand ship's maiden voyage. The newspapers had been full of stories and pictures of its luxurious accommodations. She had read boasts from the White Star Line that the Titanic was unsinkable, even going as far as saying that God Himself could not sink the mighty ship.

Yet Olivia had seen pictures of it encrusted with coral and rotting away at the bottom of the ocean.

"I can't change anything." Olivia whispered to herself, remembering Chuck's warning. What she had done-- jumping forward then back in time-- was unnatural. Changing even the smallest thing now could throw the whole universe off track.

Olivia bit her lip nervously, suddenly feeling an overwhelming weight of responsibility upon her shoulders. It was a lot to ask of a twelve-year-old girl—maybe even too much. When her mother had died last year, Olivia had been forced to grow up almost overnight. Since then, she had begun to feel that she could handle almost anything on her own. The thought of all of those people dying, though…

"If you try to stop it, a lot more may die." Olivia said to herself, pulling her knees up against her chest as she settled into her overstuffed homemade mattress.

She looked down at her hands, still trying to rub some feeling into her dead right hand. Looking at her plain and unpainted fingernails, she remembered how Evie's had looked so beautiful, manicured and painted red.

She tried again to move the fingers of her right hand, but there wasn't even the smallest sensation or response from it. She wondered if this was some strange side-effect of time travel. She began to worry that if she didn't start to get some feeling into it, that her hand would just shrivel up and die like a blackened cornhusk.

Oddly, that particular hand was the hand that Evie had used to write messages to her.

Considering this for a moment, an idea came to Olivia that made her stomach flutter. Jumping up, she almost broke her tiny mirror as she threw open the lid of her steamer trunk with excitement. She rummaged through her old clothes until she found a stub of an old lead pencil and some water-stained scraps of yellowed paper. With growing anticipation, she settled back onto her mattress and positioned the pencil stub between the limp fingers of her right hand.

Carefully, she laid it against the paper with the tip of the pencil barely touching it.

"Evie?" she called out. "Evie? Are you here with me? Did you come back with me somehow?"

Olivia's heart pounded as she watched the tip of the pencil. She held her breath, waiting for a response as she struggled to keep her arm relaxed and still.

Olivia's gasped when the pencil made a faint scratch across the paper, but then realized that the ship had rolled to the side slightly and made her arm move.

She tried to concentrate... *Please, Evie. Don't be dead. I hope that you came through with me. Please don't really be dead.*

The ship swayed again and Olivia let out a scream as the open lid of her steamer trunk clapped closed suddenly. The tapping in the next room stopped for a moment and she heard Harold call hesitantly through the wall. "You alright in there, Olive Oil?"

Olivia looked back down at the unmarked paper sheepishly. "Yes! Sorry." she called. "Thought I saw a rat. False alarm."

Faintly, she heard Harold chuckle to himself and a few seconds later the tapping resumed.

Getting herself back under control, Olivia tried again. This time, she forced herself to take slow, steady breaths and clear her mind completely as she waited for Evie to respond.

She sat very, very still for a long time, clearing her mind of glass elevators and helicopters and cell phones and computers. She felt the steady thrum of the ship beneath her and in the walls around her. She felt the sway of the Carpathia as she cut through the waves of the Atlantic. She felt the safe, calming presence of her father, who was here on the ship with her now and not an impossible distance of a hundred years past. She felt her own legs and skin and ran her own tongue over her own teeth.

Eventually, her forced breathing became a slow, steady rhythm of its own and before she even knew what was happening, Olivia drifted off to sleep.

Olivia awoke in Evie's apartment.

At least, that's where she thought she was when she first opened her eyes to the bright service light above. After a few moments of sleepy disorientation, she felt the ship's steady thrum beneath her and she realized that she was lying sideways on her linen-stuffed mattress with her feet hanging off onto the metal floor.

She didn't remember falling asleep, and when everything came rushing back to her, she looked down at the paper that had gotten pushed partly beneath her sheets as she had slept. Anxiously she snatched it up, and her heart sank when she saw that it was still blank on both sides. If Evie had come through with her somehow, then she certainly would have been able to write while Olivia had slept.

Experimentally, Olivia lifted up her numb right hand. She still was not able to move the fingers, but she could now feel a faint prickling sensation needling through it… almost as if her hand had fallen asleep and was slowly waking up. She massaged it worriedly, not liking the feeling of the useless hand and wondering if she should try to go and see Dr. Blackmarr about it.

Then she turned to the little wind-up clock that was beside her mattress and she saw that it was after eight already.

Daddy!

Without even stopping to pull on her shoes, Olivia jumped up (almost hitting her head on the low pipes above) and rushed out.

For the moment, everything else was forgotten.

Chapter Seventeen

"I told you that you're not supposed to be down here!" Curly Reynolds growled at Olivia when he saw her peeking into the empty break room. His entire misshapen, bald head was covered in black soot, making him look more like a storybook troll than ever. His angry and bloodshot eyes narrowed at her beneath his furrowed, bushy eyebrows.

Olivia peered past him at the empty break room, still hoping to catch some glimpse of her father.

"His shift ended an hour ago." Curly snarled. "Those guys already hit the bunks by now. Now beat it, bilge rat. Get out of my boiler room."

Olivia's heart sank, and she slipped back out towards the stairwell without argument. Unbidden, hot tears welled up in her eyes and she made sure she turned away quickly so Curly wouldn't see her cry. It had been days since she had seen her father and although she knew he was nearby, the desperate ache in her chest was stronger than ever.

She was about to climb the ladder back up when an impulse of defiance swept over her. Swallowing her fear of Curley and his giant boots, Olivia ducked into a service door that she knew would lead her directly to the firemen quarters.

She found the right corridor and hurried, barefoot, past the open doors where many of the men were still awake and smoking, drinking, or playing cards. Other doors were closed tight as some of the men tried to catch some sleep. Carefully, she approached the closed door of the cabin her father shared with three others. She put her ear to the door and heard nothing from inside, so she carefully cracked it open and saw that it was dark. The bunks were full and someone was snoring loudly in the darkness.

Knowing that she shouldn't Olivia crept into the room anyway, overwhelmed by the need to see her father after all of this time.

She found him in his bunk and discovered that the loud snoring was coming from him. She couldn't help but smile to herself, remembering how her mother had teased him often about his "water buffalo" snores at night. She leaned in close and could smell the soap that he had used when he had cleaned up after his shift, but also the unmistakable odors of fire and ash and coal that were so saturated in his skin that they could never be completely washed away.

She felt a triumphant surge of joy wash over her. As overwhelming and terrifying as everything had been, she was with him now and that made all the difference. She kissed him lightly on the cheek and his snoring sputtered for a moment as he mumbled something in his sleep, then it resumed again, even louder than before.

Feeling rejuvenated by her visit, Olivia slipped through the darkness again and back out the door.

Olivia arrived late for breakfast and was able to just barely scrape enough oatmeal from the bottom of the pot to halfway fill a bowl for herself.

In the crew mess hall, there were a few stewards and maids catching a break between shifts, but most of the tables were empty now.

Olivia noticed Father Saunders, the priest that worked with the first and second class passengers, eating alone and reading his Bible at one table. On an impulse, she went to join him.

Father Saunders was a short, round man with grey hair and twinkling blue eyes. He had that sort of friendly, yet sober demeanor that made people often seek out his advice. When Olivia sat across from him, he looked up at her and smiled in surprise.

"Miss Grace. Good morning to you! How does this Lord's day find you?"

Olivia smiled politely. "Very well, thank you Father Saunders."

He seemed genuinely happy to hear this. "Wonderful!" he said. "And how is your father doing?"

"He's off shift now." Olivia said. "Sleeping."

Father Saunders nodded soberly. "Bless him and all like him who toil so mightily to make this big wedge of steel move. His job is a burden to bear, for sure."

"It is." Olivia agreed, happy that the old priest appreciated the work her father had to do.

She took a few bites of her oatmeal as Father Saunders resumed reading his Bible. She had some heavy questions weighing on her mind, but she wasn't quite sure how to breach the subject with the old priest.

Finally, she just charged ahead.

"Father Saunders, do you believe that some things are meant to happen... no matter what?"

Saunders lifted his head from his reading and examined Olivia carefully. "Well, most certainly. The Bible tells us of

119

many things that were destined to happen. The birth of Jesus Christ was foretold by prophets for centuries."

Olivia considered this. "And those people... the prophets. They knew the future, right? They knew what was going to happen before it did?"

Father Saunders nodded. "That's right. God revealed a part of His plan to them so that they could prepare the world for His coming."

Olivia bit her lip thoughtfully. She couldn't help but wonder how exactly God had revealed the future to these prophets. Could they have somehow been time travelers like herself? She knew what was going to happen in the world for the next hundred years. Did that make her a prophet?

She hesitated. "You said that God revealed part of His plan. So does that mean that there is... like... one overall plan for history? Do you think that God has a set way that things are *supposed* to happen and that we shouldn't really mess with it?"

Saunders laughed lightly to himself. "Mankind has done his best to 'mess with' God's plans for all of history." He chuckled ruefully, shaking his head. "But to answer your question: yes. God most certainly does have a plan for all of us. I also happen to believe that there are events that He has planned that cannot be altered. If God really wants something to happen, then there is nothing in heaven or on Earth that can prevent it."

"Oh." Olivia responded, a little crestfallen.

"That's not to say that every moment has an unalterable outcome." Father Saunders continued. "For the most part, I think that God shows us what he wants, but that every person has their own free will and can choose whether or not to follow the path that the Lord has set for them."

Olivia considered this. "So... if people can make their own choices, then things can be changed, right?"

Saunders smiled knowingly. "You are asking some of the same questions that the greatest minds in the world have pondered for thousands of years." he rubbed his chin for a moment, as if gathering his thoughts. "Some believe that man's free will makes a predetermined future impossible. They say that if people can truly make their own choices, then who knows what's going to happen, right? I decided that I wanted to eat a second bowl of oatmeal this morning—even though I shouldn't have, mind you." he patted his wide stomach with a wink. "So if I decided that on my own, then how could it have been predetermined? How could that have already been planned by God? I could have made the wiser decision to stop at one bowl and then my fate would have been different, right? Since people are always changing their minds about things, it seems like it would be impossible to know the future, right?"

Olivia nodded. "Right! Exactly!"

Olivia remembered Chuck describing HistCorp' attempts to look into the future. *"The feeds we get from the future wormholes are just an incomprehensible blur of constantly changing images. The further away in the future it is, the more random and indecipherable it gets"*

Saunders went on. "Well, others say that even though people can make their own choices, God *already knows* what choices they will make before they even make them. That would mean that even though we have free will, God already knows what our destinies hold."

Olivia furrowed her eyebrows thoughtfully. "So our choices don't really change things after all? If something was supposed to happen, then no matter what you did to try and stop it, it would still happen?"

Father Saunders shrugged. "Like I said, it's a mystery that great minds have pondered for ages."

Olivia wasn't sure she liked the sound of that. It made her feel helpless. She prodded her oatmeal thoughtfully. "So... when bad things happen... is that part of God's plan as well?"

Saunders looked at Olivia with a gentle sadness in his eyes. "Are you thinking about your mother, dear?"

Actually, Olivia had not considered that. "Yes." she said. "That's a perfect example. What about the accident that killed my mother. Was that a part of God's plan?"

Saunders leaned forward and watched her eyes intently. "The Bible tells us that God watches over us and that everything that He does is to help us in some way. Romans 8:28 says that all things work for good to those that love God. His grand plan is too elaborate for us to see and understand, but we must have faith that everything that happens—even bad things-- happen for a reason that will eventually lead us to the greater good."

Olivia mulled this over for a moment, trying to push away the images of Evie and Chuck getting shot... of the wars that she knew were soon in store for the world around her... and of the terrible fate of the Titanic on April 14th.

"What about time travel?" Olivia asked.

Father Saunders raised his eyebrows at her, taken aback by this seemingly random change in subject. "What about it?"

"What if you could go back in time and change things?"

Saunders looked at Olivia kindly and lowered his voice. "Olivia, dear. There is nothing you could have done to prevent your mother's death. We must accept the inscrutable path that God has presented for us to follow. As tragic as it was, God had a reason for it and now your mother is with Him in His heavenly kingdom."

Olivia swallowed, not looking up to meet his eyes. "I know that. I was just wondering... you know... if time travel were real. If you could go back and change something, would that... destroy the universe?"

Saunders looked startled. "Dear me! What a notion! Why would it destroy the universe?"

Olivia hesitated. "If God had a plan and everything happens for a reason, then he wouldn't want you to change it, would he? He wouldn't allow that to happen, right?"

Father Saunders shook his head. "Something like time travel wouldn't ever happen without God allowing it to happen in the first place. If it were actually possible for someone to go back in time, then that, too, would be God's will. If you could somehow change the course of history, then it would be what God had intended all along."

Chapter Eighteen

"If you could somehow change the course of history, then it would be what God had intended all along."

Father Saunders' words played through Olivia's troubled thoughts throughout the rest of the morning. By the time the sun was at its peak, Olivia was huddled on a teak deck chair on the uppermost deck, squinting in the bright sunshine with her legs pulled up against her as the cool, salty air whipped her hair around her face. Couples and families strolled the deck, looking out at the rolling blue waves that stretched to the horizon in every direction.

On the forward deck, Olivia saw a small cluster of officers... Captain Rostron among them. Each of them were using a sextant to take noontime bearings and jotting down their calculations. They would compare their results and then be able to determine exactly where they were. The Carpathia held a daily sweepstakes for its passengers, who all made bets on how many miles the ship had travelled since the previous day. It wasn't a lot of money, but it was enough to make it an entertaining diversion. As Olivia watched the officers, she couldn't help but imagine Captain Smith and his officers onboard the Titanic, taking their own bearings and unknowingly steering that enormous ocean liner and all of its passengers towards their approaching doom.

It was April 12.

Olivia rubbed her hand absently as she struggled with her thoughts.

Even if she tried, could she really change history? She was only a kid, after all. What could she possibly do that would save those thousands of doomed people? And then... what about the warnings that Chuck had given her about paradoxes and the dangers of making changes? Could she really break the universe? Would her actions be like throwing a wrench into the finely-tuned machinery that kept everything running smoothly?

These thoughts plagued Olivia's mind for hours... and it was a banana hitting her on the side of the head that finally brought her out of her cloud.

She flinched as it fell into her lap and looked up in time to see Bubs dragging a chair up beside her.

"Catch." he said too late, smiling at her with a mischievous grin.

Olivia rubbed her ear and glared at him. "If you poke a tiger with a stick, Bubs, you should be prepared to get mauled."

"It's not a stick, it's a banana." he grinned, sitting down nearby. "What's with all of the skipped meals, lately? You trying to lose some weight?"

Olivia blinked at him. "What skipped meals?"

Bubs bit into his own half-eaten banana. "It's three o'clock! They stopped serving lunch two hours ago."

Olivia squinted up at the bright afternoon sky in surprise. "Really? It's that late already?"

Bubs guffawed. "You keep acting like your mind is a hundred miles away!"

"More like a hundred years." Olivia mumbled.

"What's gotten into you lately?"

Olivia shook her head quietly. "I just... I have some decisions to make."

"You sound like a grown-up." Bubs complained, then he snapped his fingers. "Oh, hey! You know that guy in second class that I told you was a jewel thief! Well get this: the guy won't even let anyone in to clean his room! No sheets turned down, no fresh towels. He just keeps his room locked up and tells everyone to stay out."

"Hmmm..." Olivia murmured distractedly as she peeled her banana.

"Don't you see?" Bubs said with exasperation. "The guy is definitely hiding something! He won't even leave his room because he's afraid someone's going to find his stash!"

Olivia bit into her banana, staring out at the blue horizon. "Umm-hmm." she muttered.

"Is that all you have to say?" Bubs pressed. "This is big stuff here! Nothing exciting ever happens on this ship. This is our chance for an adventure!"

Olivia heard approaching voices and looked up to see two women strolling up the deck towards them. They were passengers—probably first class by the looks of their elaborate dresses. The younger of the two was trying to hold a parasol against the headwind and it whipped and pulled like a wild chicken trying to break free from her grasp.

The older woman wore a netted dress hat that she was struggling to hold in place with her hand. Both of them seemed startled by how windy the upper deck was and were trying to maintain their composure while at the same time hurrying for the nearest stairwell to find cover.

As they passed close by, Olivia saw that the older woman was wearing a bright orange-and-black striped scarf. It was an odd fashion choice that clashed terribly with the rest of her clothing, and to make matters worse, the scarf, too, was whipping around in the wind as if trying to break free from her neck or strangle her in the process.

When Olivia saw the scarf, a picture came into her head as clear as if she were looking at it in front of her. She saw the Titanic survivors, huddled, dazed, and cold, crowding the decks of the Carpathia on the morning after the tragedy. She saw this woman handing a blanket to one of them, and she remembered this very scarf around her neck. It had been black-and-white, but the pattern was unmistakable.

"I saw a picture of that scarf." Olivia said to herself in amazement as the women passed.

Bubs looked bewildered. "A picture? Of *that* scarf? You mean in a catalog or something?"

"A hundred years from now, when people read about the Carpathia and the Titanic, they will see a picture of that woman in that scarf on April 15th."

Bubs was definitely getting worried now. He looked from her faraway expression to the old woman's scarf, then back again. "What on Earth are you talking 'bout Olivia?"

But Olivia felt something building up inside her now... a sort of reckless resolve that made her jump to her feet before she even realized exactly what it was she was going to do. She found herself running up behind the two women after they had passed and catching them just before they reached the stairwell.

"Excuse me, mam?" Olivia asked loudly.

The two women turned around. The younger one was still struggling to keep the parasol in her hands from getting stolen away by the wind and the old woman was valiantly keeping her hat pinned to her head with the palm of her hand. When they saw Olivia, they looked at her with mild annoyance, eying the shelter of the nearby stairwell that they had been trying to reach.

"What is it young lady?" the old woman prompted irritably.

Olivia held her breath, realizing that she was about to do something reckless and terrifying. She looked at the old woman apologetically. "Please realize, 'mam, that what I'm about to do, I'm very sorry for."

The women both looked at her, baffled. "Sorry for what?" the younger woman asked impatiently.

Then, steeling her courage and holding her breath, Olivia reached out and snatched away the older woman's scarf suddenly. The old woman's eyes went wide as Olivia tossed the scarf up in the air where it was snatched away instantly by the wind, disappearing from sight.

The two women yelled out in protest, but Olivia didn't even hear them. She dropped to the deck, closing her eyes tightly and yelling out in anticipation of the cataclysm that her reckless action would trigger. She huddled up into a ball at the women's feet, cringing and waiting for the universe to come to a sputtering stop around her and fall completely to pieces.

After a terrifying moment, the universe seemed to still be intact.

Olivia slowly opened her eyes and looked up at the shocked and offended glares of the two women standing above her.

"I… I did it!" Olivia said with wonder. "The universe didn't end!"

The women were definitely looking at Olivia now as if she was a patient who had escaped from an asylum. "Young lady how dare you---"

But Olivia didn't even hear the angry woman's outrage. Her mind was suddenly filled with the new possibilities that had just opened before her.

"I have changed history." she said in amazement, looking up at the outraged woman. "A hundred years from now, there won't be a picture of you wearing that scarf on April 15th. The scarf is gone! I've actually changed something!"

"What is your name, young lady? I demand that you---"

Olivia turned her back on the women and wandered back up the deck, feeling the wind in her face and the burden of indecision lifted from her mind. As she passed Bubs, he stared at her in open-mouthed shock, a bit of half-chewed banana on his tongue. He swallowed it and jumped up to walk beside her. "You feelin okay?" he said worriedly. "Maybe we should go and see Dr. Blackmarr."

"I'm feeling *great*, Bubs!" Olivia nearly shouted, taking a deep breath of the salty air. "I know now what I've got to do."

Bubs glanced back at the two gaping women. "Let me guess. You're going to knit that old lady a new scarf?"

Olivia stopped and turned to him with a fiery determination in her eyes. "Bubs, you said you wanted to have an adventure, right?"

Bubs looked at her warily. "Did I say that?"

"I've got some things to tell you." she said. "Now that I know that the universe will let us, we're going to change history."

The Universe, however, was not so easily thwarted.

The two women watched in astonished outrage as the impertinent little girl strolled away from them, joined now by a little street-rat of a boy who was no doubt her partner in this unprovoked assault.

They stood at the top of the stairwell, torn between chasing after her or finally retreating into the shelter of the stairs. It was the parasol that made up their minds for them. Finally losing its battle with the brutal wind, the lacy umbrella collapsed and folded upwards upon itself. The women both looked at it, startled, and hurried out of the headwind and towards the relative shelter of the lower decks.

They were about to go back inside when the younger woman pulled at her mother's arm. "Mama, look!"

The old woman turned to see a whitewashed steel lifeboat crane towering nearby. Wrapped up in its tangle of girders and cables, within arm's reach, the black and orange scarf fluttered in the breeze.

The younger woman reached up and retrieved it for her mother. "Here you go, Mama!" she smiled.

The old woman took the scarf and wrapped it back around her neck, still incensed that it had been taken in the first place.

Chapter Nineteen

Olivia had considered that her story might have been too fantastic for Bubs to even digest. She was just going to tell him what she knew about the Titanic without mentioning HistCorp or anything else... but in the end something compelled her to tell him everything. She talked for almost an hour... telling him about her trip to the future New York City, the strange truth about wormholes and quantum theory, and ending finally with the horrible deaths of Chuck and Evie in a field beneath the starry sky.

There was a huge relief in just telling him... just to let someone else know everything that she had been through. Remarkably, Bubs listened without interrupting, his expression unreadable throughout. It was only when Olivia finished, nearly out of breath, that she watched him in silence and waited to see what his reaction would be to her startling tale.

Bubs watched her wordlessly for so long that she had to finally prompt him to say something. "Well?" she asked him impatiently.

He blinked. "Well what?"

"Don't you have anything to say?"

They were in the empty crew mess hall, sitting at the same table Olivia and Father Saunders had been sitting at during breakfast. Bubs pulled his oversized sleeves up his arms and propped his elbows up onto the wooden table. "It's a great story." Bubs shrugged.

Olivia leaned forward. "It's not a story, Bubs. It happened. You saw the wormhole, too. You heard it."

Bubs curled his lip. "Right. I did. I left and then came back four minutes later and you were still on the deck. You hadn't gone anywhere."

Olivia shook her head. "My body was still here. But I was gone for three days, Bubs. I really need you to believe me."

"Why?" Bubs asked.

Olivia took a deep breath. *Why?* She didn't understand herself why it was so desperately important to her at that moment.

"I guess it's because I can't do this alone." she said finally.

"Do what alone, Olivia? What exactly are you planning to do?"

Olivia lowered her voice and looked at him seriously. "I'm going to change history." she said.

"How?" he asked her.

Olivia watched him firmly. "First, I have to know that you believe me."

Bubs met her gaze for a moment, then finally shrugged. "Alright. Sure."

Olivia blinked. "Really?"

The corner of Bub's mouth twisted into a grin. "No. Not really. I actually think that you're crazy. But... you know what? I've been itching for something exciting to happen around here and it sounds like you're about to really stir things up so... whatever you're doing... count me in."

Olivia opened her mouth to say something else, but after looking at Bubs' anxious grin, she decided that she would have to take what she could get for now.

"So..." Bubs continued. "Is it actually 'changing history' if it hasn't even happened yet?"

"It's going to happen." Olivia said. "On the night of April 14th, at 11:40 pm, the Titanic is going to hit an iceberg. By 2:20 am, the entire ship will be underwater and one thousand, five hundred and twenty-three men, women, and children are going to die."

Bubs paled slightly and swallowed, perhaps just realizing the full horror of something so devastating. He cleared his throat. "Well... all right. Then how are you going to stop it? How do we keep the Titanic away from that berg?"

Olivia hesitated. "I don't think we can, actually."

Bubs looked flabbergasted. "Say what?"

"We're not on the Titanic and we're probably not going to be able to stop it from hitting the iceberg. I've played it over in my mind a thousand times and just about the only thing we can do right now is have Harold warn them about the iceberg with his wireless set. He's the only one that can reach them."

Bubs nodded. "Well, great! Then let's do that."

Olivia shook her head. "The problem is... even if we could convince Harold that we somehow knew that there was an iceberg there and get him to warn the Titanic... it still wouldn't change things. The Titanic was already warned about ice in its path. The Carpathia and lots of other ships all around sent warnings just like it. The captain knew the danger but they steamed on full speed ahead anyway."

Bubs looked confused. "If they won't listen to us, then what else can we do?"

"I've been asking myself the same thing." Olivia said thoughtfully. "We can't stop the Titanic, but we can try to do something here, on the Carpathia."

"Like what?"

Olivia reached into her layers of clothes and pulled out a scrap of paper that she had hidden there. She laid it out on the table between them to reveal a crude map that she had drawn after breakfast.

"This is where the Titanic strikes the iceberg." Olivia said, pointing at a spot on the map that she had marked with a big, bold "X" mark. "She's headed west towards New York and is three days out from her last stop in Queenstown."

Bubs nodded as Olivia's finger moved down the map and to the right. "Here is where the Carpathia will be when the Titanic calls for help. We're headed east and will actually pass near the crash site earlier that day. When the SOS comes, we'll be over fifty miles southeast and will need to turn around and steam hard to reach her. Still, the Carpathia can only go about 16 knots if the Captain pushes her all out... and it will take almost four hours to reach the Titanic."

Bubs looked down at the crudely drawn map with a frown. "Four hours? That will be too late, won't it? The Titanic will be gone by then."

"Right. The Titanic will be completely gone by 2:20." Olivia agreed. "We'll only get there in time to pick up about seven hundred survivors from the lifeboats. Everyone else will be dead. Unless..."

"Unless what?" Bubs prompted.

"Unless we can get there sooner."

Bubs looked again at the map. "You just said that the Carpathia can't go above 16 knots. How to you expect to get us there sooner? Are we going to fly? Are you planning on harnessing a school of dolphins and having them pull us there?"

"No... you're right. The Carpathia still can't go over 16 knots. It would most definitely take us four hours to reach the

Titanic if we were over fifty miles away. Instead, when we get that distress call on the night of April 14th... I want us to be much, much closer."

Bubs was in.

Olivia hated that he still didn't believe her whole story, but he was excited now about doing something different and she knew that he could be counted on to help in whatever way he could.

The problem was that she still didn't know exactly what they were going to do.

As Olivia lay in bed that night, the thousand moving pieces of the puzzle resolved themselves into three clear tasks that now lay before her.

To get the Carpathia closer to the Titanic, she had to somehow get the ship to slow down so they wouldn't actually pass the crash site and have to turn around again. Also, she would have to find a way to get the Carpathia much further north than their current route. Finally, there was the matter of getting the Carpathia to where the Titanic *actually* was sinking instead of where everyone would *think* she was sinking.

Olivia had read that the coordinates that the Titanic sent when she was going down were actually thirteen miles away from where she actually was. Thirteen miles was almost an hour's travel for the Carpathia... and when that fateful night came, there wouldn't be time to waste going to the wrong place. She had to somehow make the Carpathia arrive in the right place with enough time to save all of those people.

Olivia lay on her mattress staring up at the bright service light above, trying to puzzle out a solution to her seemingly impossible three tasks.

Slower. Further north. Right coordinates.
Slower. Further north. Right coordinates.

Eventually, the rhythmic tapping of Harold's wireless set through the wall began to lull her. Although she fought it, her thoughts began to slip from her grasp like wriggling fish that she couldn't hold on to… and soon after that, she drifted off to a troubled and restless sleep.

Chapter Twenty

When Olivia awoke on April 13th, her right hand tingled with the sensation of a thousand bristling needles.

Blinking away the heavy sleep from her eyes, she rubbed her numb palm and was surprised to find that she could actually feel her fingertips as she massaged it. She lifted her hand up and tried experimentally to move it. She almost cheered when her fingers gave a feeble twitch in response to her efforts.

She met with Bubs at breakfast and he seemed excited about something when he saw her. "Hey! Guess what! You know that jewel thief we had in second class? The one who wouldn't let anyone near his bags or his room?"

"Bubs, we really need to focus on—"

But he waved her quiet. "No, no. Listen to this. Jimmy the steward was walking by the guy's room last night and he heard these strange noises coming from behind the door. Like a whimpering, crying noise. He had just seen the guy in the dining hall a few minutes earlier, so he knew the room was supposed to be empty, right?"

Olivia sighed. She could see that Bubs was going to tell this story whether she tried to stop him or not. "Okay." she said. "So, what was it? A ghost?"

Bubs' eyes grew wide. "No! But that would have been a much better story! Man, I wish that had been true!"

Olivia rolled her eyes. "Well... what was it?"

Bubs hunkered down over his oatmeal, happy to have hooked her attention. "So Jimmy knocks at the door and asks who is in there and nobody answers but the crying seems to get louder and now there's like a scratching sound on the other side of the door, like someone is struggling to get out."

Bubs was smiling now, milking the story. Olivia bit her tongue impatiently and let him go on.

"So Jimmy starts to panic thinking this guy has kidnapped some poor kids or something and has had them locked up for days... so he hurries to open the door and guess what he finds!"

Olivia threw her hands up. "I don't know!"

"Dogs!" Bubs declared triumphantly.

"Dogs?"

"Dogs."

Olivia cocked her eyebrow at Bubs. "So... he was a dog smuggler?"

Bubs shrugged. "Well... sort of. I mean, they were his dogs... not stolen or anything... but he didn't want to send them down to stay in the ship's kennel like he was supposed to. He was afraid it would be too drafty for the little pooches. So he smuggled them aboard in his suitcase and was keeping them in his room. They were two tiny little things. Like two fluffs of cotton with legs and eyes."

"Hmmm..." Olivia said distractedly, taking a bite of her oatmeal. "So did Jimmy take them down to the kennel?"

Bubs shook his head. "Nope. The guy came back and he gave Jimmy a dollar if he promised not to say anything."

"And Jimmy took the dollar?"

"Who wouldn't? Jimmy said he wouldn't say anything as long as the little fur balls didn't make a mess on the floor."

Olivia actually smiled. "Well, Bubs, you were right. The guy was hiding something after all."

Bubs smiled proudly. "Told ya! And I'll tell you something else, too. I think I have an idea for getting us closer to the Titanic tomorrow night."

Olivia looked at him sharply. "What idea?"

"Engine trouble." he said simply. "You are always crawling around in these back access corridors. Let's find a great big bundle of wires somewhere and cut 'em. If we can conk out the steering or electrical or something, then we'll have to stop for repairs. If we're behind schedule by a few hours, then we won't have to turn around to steam back towards the Titanic."

Olivia shook her head. "Not a bad idea... except that if we break something then we don't know for sure how long it would take them to repair it. What if we cut the wrong wire and did so much damage that we were still dead in the water when we got the call tomorrow night? Then we wouldn't be able to get there at all."

The smile fell from Bubs' face. "Oh... right."

"Slower, further north, right coordinates." Olivia chanted under her breath.

Bubs' face clouded. "Huh?"

"We not only have to get us behind schedule a bit, but we also need to get us moving further north. Just enough to get us closer to where the collision will be."

Bubs considered this. "We could throw off the ship's rudder a bit. Make it so we drag to the north without them knowing it."

"Would you even know how to do that?" Olivia asked.

"No." Bubs admitted.

"Messing with the rudder of the ship sounds kinda risky. I want them to be able to steer us in the right direction when the time comes." Olivia reminded him.

Bubs thought for a moment. "We could sneak onto the bridge and tickle the pilot under his left arm. That would cause him to twitch and turn the wheel a little to the north."

Olivia looked at him thoughtfully. "Right. The bridge."

Bubs' eyes widened. "Um… I was just kidding about the whole tickle thing. That would never actually work. You do know that, right?"

But Olivia's mind was working now. "They have a compass up there." she said. "A big one. After the captain and the officers take the noon bearings, they rely mostly on that compass to steer for the rest of the day, right?"

"I think so." Bubs agreed.

"We don't need to mess with the ship. We just need to mess with that compass."

Bubs looked skeptical. "How do you mess with a compass?"

"The needle points to the magnetic north." Olivia said. "If we could get a magnet nearby without them knowing it, then we might be able to throw it off just enough to get us to drift a bit from our course."

Bubs considered this. "But then when the captain took the noonday bearings tomorrow, he would see that we're off course and he would correct it, right? He would turn us back south again."

"We would have to do it after the noon bearings tomorrow." Olivia agreed.

She remembered watching Captain Rostron and his officers taking the bearings yesterday, jotting down their numbers and adding up the miles they had travelled. Olivia thought about this for a moment, and the whisper of another idea began to form in her mind.

"How does that sweepstakes work?" she asked.

Bubs looked confused by the sudden change of subject. "What? The mileage sweepstakes?"

"Right."

"Um… well, you've been onboard eleven months. You know just about all there is to know about it. It's just this crazy game the passengers like to play to try and win some money. It costs a dime for a ticket. Everyone tries to make a guess at how far the ship travelled since noon the day before. After the captain takes our bearings, they gather everyone up in the first class lounge and announce our mileage. The person who guessed the closest wins all the money that was collected."

Olivia thought about this. "Does the crew ever play?"

"Sure." Bubs said. "The officers never play, of course, because it might look like they were cheating… but Jimmy the steward plays at least once a week. Last year he won a thirty-dollar pot and blew it all in the first port we pulled into."

Olivia chewed her lip thoughtfully, working out the details of a possible plan. An idea had come to her for slowing down the ship… an idea that just might work. The problem was, it meant having to make a deal with the devil.

Chapter Twenty-One

"I told you that the fires are no place for mangy little bilge rats like you! Your father doesn't even go on shift for another six hours! I'm sick of you scampering around down here and I'm going to tell the captain about it this time!"

Curly's blackened face glowered at Olivia furiously and Olivia knew that if he wasn't afraid of what her father might do to him, Curly would have hit her right then and there. She saw his bony hands trembling as if he was fighting the urge that very moment.

"I'm not here to see my father." Olivia protested. "I wanted to talk to you."

This may have been the last thing that the irate foreman ever expected her to say. Instantly, his eyes narrowed into wary slits. "Whotcha talkin 'bout, bilge rat? I got nothing to say to you."

That's funny. Olivia thought. *You always seem to have plenty to say to me...*

"I have a proposition for you." Olivia said.

"A what?" Curly growled.

"A proposition… a deal. I have an idea for a way we both might be able to make some money."

Curly sneered at her. "Nonsense! Get out of here before I crush you beneath my boots."

"No, no." Olivia protested. "Seriously. Hear me out. I've been thinking about how you are the most powerful man on this whole ship."

Curly absently rubbed the knob on the side of his bald head and continued to glare at her warily, as if expecting some trick. "Wotcha goin on about?"

"You're really the one who controls everything." Olivia said simply. "The captain may be steering and giving orders, but without you, the ship would be dead in the water. It goes nowhere without you."

Curly, though still suspicious, clearly approved of the flattery (just as Olivia had hoped he would).

"Wot's yer point?" he snapped irritably. "So I make the ship move. How's that going to earn me any money besides the pound a day Cunard pays me?"

"The sweepstakes." Olivia said.

"What?"

"The daily mileage sweepstakes." Olivia said. "Every day the passengers try to guess how—"

"I know what it is!" Curly spat. "What's it gotta do with me?"

Olivia cleared her throat. "Well… everyone knows and expects that we'll be cruising at close to 12 knots. In twenty-four hours, that should take us about 333 miles. Everybody is going to be guessing close to that number."

"So?" Curly growled.

"Well… I was thinking that you control the furnaces, so you control the speed."

"Twelve knots is our max cruising speed. Always has been." Curly said shortly.

"I'm not saying go faster." Olivia said. "I'm saying if you could make us go a little slower... say 10 and a half knots between now and noon tomorrow, then we would actually travel about fifty miles less than everyone else was expecting. With a wager in the sweepstakes, no one else would even be close. It would be a sure win."

Curly sneered at her. "And everyone would accuse me of cheating... rightfully so!"

"That's why I would place the bet for you." Olivia said. "Everyone would be so surprised and happy that a poor little girl like me won that nobody would ever question it. I could give you half the money and we'd both be a little richer for it."

Olivia could see Curly's eyes spark at the idea, then he leveled his shrewd and wary gaze at her again. "Half? It seems that I would be the one doin' all the work here... and you sure aint got a dime, so it would be my dime placing the wager. I'll give you a dollar of the winnings. That seems fair enough. More than enough to buy you a liquorish or bit of chocolate at the next port."

Now honestly Olivia didn't care about the money at all. If she could somehow just get Curly to slow down the ship and get them closer to where the Titanic would be, then she would be satisfied. The problem was, she knew that Curly would be suspicious and probably call the whole thing off if he thought her motives were anything other than getting some of the winnings.

"A dollar!" Olivia shot back with feigned indigence. "Who do you think you're dealing with? This was my idea and you can't do it without me! Thirty percent!"

The foreman rubbed his chin and watched her shiftily. "Ten." he countered.

"Twenty... and my dad gets to work furnace number two for the next three crossings... the other furnace doesn't close all the way and it makes him too hot."

Curly looked ready to hit her again. He gnashed his teeth, but finally relented. "Deal." he said, then dug into his pockets and pulled out a dirty dime. "You place the bet and I'll take care of the rest."

Olivia felt a rush of elation, unable to believe that she had accomplished something so monumental.

"Ten and a half knots." Olivia reminded him.

"I'll take care of it!" Curly hissed. "Just bring me my money tomorrow!"

Despite her elation, Olivia couldn't help but feel a sickening nervousness as she made her way to the purser's office to buy the sweepstakes ticket.

Although she knew that what she was doing could possibly save over a thousand lives, it also made her sick to her stomach that she was doing something dishonest... and that she had to work with Curly to do it.

She carried the filthy dime in her hand with two fingers, holding it the whole way like it was a dead rat in her grasp. The sooner she got rid of it, the better.

When she reached the purser's desk, she found that Bubs' father, the assistant purser, was on duty. For some reason, this made Olivia hesitate. She was overwhelmed with the guilty urge to turn and run, but before she could make a dash for it, he looked up and saw her standing there.

"Olivia! Hello!" he smiled at her cordially.

Olivia paused, half turned to run, with the dirty dime dangling between her fingers. She swallowed, and hesitantly returned his smile. "Hello Mr. Glasser."

"You and Bubs staying out of trouble today?"

Olivia nodded. "Yessir... although I haven't seen him since breakfast."

Mr. Glasser winced. "Ooo... that's a lot of time for him to get into trouble on his own, isn't it?"

"Yessir, it is." Olivia smiled.

"Well, what is it I can do for you today?"

Olivia cleared her throat nervously, then plunged forward. "I would like to play the sweepstakes, please."

Mr. Glasser raised his eyebrows in surprise. "Really?"

"Yessir. I've... um... been saving this dime and I think I would like to give it a try." She placed the grimy coin on the purser's desk carefully.

Mr. Glasser looked at it for a moment, then back up to her. "Olivia, dear. I know that your father works very hard for every penny he makes. Are you sure you want to waste this on a wager? How would he feel about that?"

Olivia's stomach tightened with guilt. "Oh, he... um... he said it was okay with him." she lied uneasily.

Mr. Glasser looked at her for another moment, but didn't argue. Finally, he reached into a drawer and pulled out a paper ticket. "Alright." he said. "You've got one ticket then. Make it count."

"Right." Olivia said nervously. "Thank you, sir."

He picked up a pencil and wrote out her name carefully on the ticket. "So you need to guess how far you think the ship is going to travel between noon today and noon tomorrow."

"Yessir. I would like to guess 290 miles sir."

Mr. Glasser's pencil hovered above the ticket hesitantly, then he looked up at her. "Um... Olivia dear... are you sure about that?" he looked around and lowered his voice to her. "You might be better off choosing something a little... higher. Maybe between 320 and 350?"

"Thank you sir. No, I'm positive. 290 please."

Mr. Glasser looked ready to protest, but bit his tongue. "Fine. Alright. I'll place your bet for you if you're certain that's the number you want, Olivia."

"Thank you Mr. Glasser." Olivia said with relief.

"Listen for the whistle tomorrow afternoon then come up to the first class lounge to hear who the winner is. I wish you luck."

"Thanks!" Olivia smiled, then she turned and started back down the nearby stairs. In her mind, she saw her three tasks looming (*slower, further north, right coordinates*) and it was a huge relief to realize that at least one of them was close to being taken care of.

Chapter Twenty-Two

Near midnight that night, Olivia was up on the top deck with her mind a turbulent storm of thoughts and fears.

She knew she should try to get some sleep, but the uneasy worries churning through her head refused to let her rest. It was now less than twenty-four hours before the Titanic was supposed to hit an iceberg somewhere out there in the dark water.

Olivia looked out at the gently rolling waves of the Atlantic beneath the starry sky. She imagined the Titanic steaming through these waters, lit up brightly with a hundred blazing electric lights... and she imagined somewhere in its path the mountainous iceberg, drifting silently in the darkness... an enormous frozen mass that was destined to make history.

In the silence, Olivia could hear the white water churning below as the Carpathia cut through the waves. The cold wind blew as furiously as ever here on the top deck, and to Olivia it seemed that the big ship was moving as fast as always. She hoped that Curly was doing his part, though, slowing them down just enough to make that critical difference. There was nothing she could do about it now, so Olivia had to force her mind to let those tense thoughts go.

Tomorrow would be the big day. She would check off the other two things on her list, and if all went well, they would be in the right place at the right time.

Olivia was startled out of her thoughts by someone coming up beside her. She turned and let out a gasp when she saw that it was the old woman she had encountered the day before. Despite the cold night air, the frail old lady was barefoot and wearing nothing more than a thin nightdress and--- this is the part that horrified Olivia--- that orange and black striped scarf around her neck.

"It looks cold out here." the old woman commented conversationally as she leaned against the railing beside Olivia and looked out over the starry sky.

Olivia's mouth had gone dry as she stared at the woman with sickening alarm. "But I changed history." Olivia whispered in horror. "I got rid of that scarf."

The old woman smiled at her with a playful gleam in her eyes. "What? Oh, right! This was *the* scarf, wasn't it? What a delightful coincidence that I grabbed this on my way out. A lovely bit of irony that I would love to take credit for, but I must admit I wore it only because I thought it might be chilly. Oddly enough, it turns out I can't feel a thing." she laughed lightly. "Isn't that strange? Quite an unexpected side-effect."

Olivia could clearly see goose bumps dimpling the old woman's wrinkled arm and she knew that the woman had to be freezing right now.

The old woman took a deep breath of the salty air as it whipped her grey hair around her face. "What a beautiful night." she said. "Look how clear and calm it is out there. Just amazing. It's hard to believe that the waters just a hundred miles north of here are so deadly."

"What do you mean?" Olivia asked carefully, feeling a superstitious shiver at this whole encounter. Her eyes darted again to the orange and black scarf, which whipped about in the wind like a live snake around the woman's neck.

"Well, icebergs of course." the old woman smiled. "Like the one that's going to sink the Titanic tomorrow night."

The old lady turned her eyes towards Olivia knowingly and gave her a sparkling smile.

"I never lose, Miss Grace." the old woman continued. "You really should have known that about me. You cannot run from me and you cannot hide... not in Mr. Ferryman's basement, not in a park, and not in the past. I will find you again and again and I will always... *always* get what I want."

Olivia's mouth tried to move, but she found herself unable to do or say anything... petrified in shock and terror.

"Dumas? Minerva Dumas?" she choked out incredulously.

The old woman raised her eyebrow, then lifted up her bony hands to examine them in the starlight. "Your accidental little jaunt into the future really opened up a lot of new doors for us, Miss Grace. HistCorp has created five new sections dedicated solely to researching how you managed to do it. After several years and despite the best efforts of Mr. Ferryman to throw us off track, we have made some significant breakthroughs. So... here I am."

Olivia's mouth had gone dry.

"Well..." Dumas corrected. "I'm not technically here at all, I suppose. The wormhole I used came out in cabin 617, which happened to be where this withered old hag was sleeping. She had a close enough genetic match to mine to let me 'borrow' her body while she slept." She lifted her arms out to the wind. "Curious that I can't feel the cold, isn't it? In every other way it feels as if I'm actually here."

"Did you say that Chuck is alive?" Olivia breathed.

Dumas lifted the old woman's eyes up to her. "Hmmm? Oh, quite right. Yes, Ferryman is alive, thanks to a

150

considerable amount of time and money spent on his recovery. Once we saved his life, you would have thought he would have tried harder to help us replicate your miraculous journey. Instead, he was stubbornly unhelpful."

"His life wouldn't have needed saving if your men hadn't shot him in the first place!" Olivia countered angrily.

"Details." the old woman waved dismissively. "Now that we're finally on the right track, it seems that keeping him alive is no longer as important as it once was." She leveled a meaningful glance at Olivia.

Olivia felt a helpless panic. "Don't hurt him!" she demanded above the wind.

"Well that..." Dumas said in the old woman's voice, "is all up to you now, isn't it?"

Olivia glared at her. "What do you mean?"

Dumas crossed her bony arms and turned to face Olivia. "We've been watching you, Miss Grace. Quite closely, actually, since the moment you returned. We see what you are trying to do and... although this scarf stubbornly held on for a little longer... your efforts are changing the course of history."

Olivia blinked. "They are?"

"Miss Grace, you changed history the moment you glimpsed the future. Everything is different now."

As if to illustrate her point, Dumas unwrapped the scarf from her neck and threw it out over the side of the ship. Olivia watched it fall to the black water below and disappear into the darkness behind them. "Changing history, it turns out, is rather easy. Guiding the course of history the way you want it to go... well... it turns out that's a bit harder. Whenever you pull one string here in the past, you never know what you're dislodging in the future. It's all very unstable. We're still not even sure what's going to happen tomorrow night. Since you came back, many of our wormholes to the past have become just as garbled and unclear as those looking into the future. It is quite... frustrating."

The old woman took a deep breath of the cold night air again. Her arms were turning blue, but she still seemed unaffected by it. "Of course," she continued lightly. "The easiest solution to this would be for me to just kill you right now."

Olivia inhaled sharply, feeling her heart pounding heavily in her chest.

"Having you mucking around here in the past is far too dangerous." Dumas continued. "I'm quite satisfied with the future I've made for myself and I don't like the idea of you poking around back here where you might knock something loose and change it all. What I should do is just toss you into the black water like that scarf. I should put an end to this right here and now."

Olivia tensed and gripped the cold steel rail tightly. "Why haven't you?" she asked shakily.

"I want something." Dumas said after a moment's pause. "And I need you to get it for me."

Olivia swallowed. "What?" she asked hoarsely.

The old woman's grey eyes flashed shrewdly at her. "The RMS Titanic is carrying the transatlantic mail to America. Among the packages and parcels being transported is one in particular… a small package addressed to a Mr. Clive Arogia of Boston. I want that package, Miss Grace."

Olivia carefully pushed her hair from her eyes as it whipped about in the wind. "What's that got to do with me?"

"You, Miss Grace, are going to go aboard the Titanic and get it. It will be in the mail room, in a bag already sorted for shipment to Boston upon arrival. A small plainly-wrapped brown package."

Olivia was horrified. "You have got to be kidding me! You want me to go aboard the ship while it's sinking? Why don't you do it yourself?"

Dumas smiled wryly. "Even if old witherbones here was fifty years younger and capable of such a thing, I'm going to get kicked out of her body the moment she wakes up. It just wouldn't do for a loud noise to startle her awake knee deep in water on a sinking ship. It's going to have to be you. I want you to retrieve the package, and then you're going to put it in a bank vault when you return to New York. You'll deposit it at the Wall Street branch of the New England Savings and Loan under the name M. Dumas."

"What could be so important?" Olivia countered. "Is it gold? Diamonds?"

Dumas cracked a smile showing rows of yellowed teeth in the old woman's mouth. "You really don't know me at all, do you, dearie? No, no… I am already the richest woman in the world. It's no longer about money for me… it's all about the power now. One can never quite have enough power."

Olivia swallowed down a lump that was rising in her throat. "I think you've got too much power as it is. I don't think I want to do anything to make you even stronger."

The old woman smiled and shrugged. "Fine. Then your friend Chuck will die. Oh… and it's also possible that one of the men sharing a bunk with your father may 'sleepwalk' one night and accidentally stab him in the throat. People do the craziest thing while they're sleeping sometimes." Dumas winked the old woman's grey eyes and a cold shiver snaked up Olivia's spine.

"You wouldn't…" Olivia gasped.

"Oh I most certainly would. Did I not mention that I hate to lose, Miss Grace?"

Olivia stared at the old woman, meeting her gaze for a long, terrible moment as she struggled with what to do.

"How do you know we're even going to make it in time?" Olivia asked at last.

Dumas shrugged. "I don't. I'm betting, though, that you're going to do everything you can to get there before that big ship slips under. Lives are depending on you... and I don't just mean those poor souls onboard the Titanic."

Olivia stared wordlessly at Dumas, feeling terrified and trapped. She had never in her life encountered anyone so evil and it was nearly paralyzing.

"Just remember," Dumas smiled. "I'll be watching you and…"

She trailed off in mid-sentence and suddenly frowned. Her forehead creased in confusion and a moment later, her bony arms went up around her and she began to shiver uncontrollably. Olivia watched as those grey eyes grew wide in alarm as they looked around at the deck and the open sky above, then her gaze focused again on Olivia.

"You!" the woman muttered weakly as confused recognition crossed her face.

Suddenly, her frail legs buckled beneath her and instinctively, Olivia lunged forward and caught her before she fell. The woman frowned worriedly. "How did I get out of bed?" she murmured. "What's happened?"

"It's alright." Olivia said quietly, trying to sound calm even though her own heartbeat was still thrumming wildly in her ears. "You were just sleepwalking. Come on, I'll help you back to your cabin."

The woman looked at Olivia hesitantly, then put her arm around Olivia's shoulder. "Thank you, child." she said, and let herself be supported as Olivia led her back inside.

Chapter Twenty-Three

Olivia was too shaken to even try to sleep for the rest of that night. She remained in her tiny little cubbyhole for the next few hours, listening to the creaking and groaning of the sleeping ship as it sped through the water. Dumas' creepy midnight visit in the old woman's body had been beyond terrifying, and Olivia found herself unable to do much more than stare at the blank white wall for several hours afterwards as she struggled to regain her composure.

At 7:30 on the morning of April 14, Olivia was sitting in Harold's office next door.

His room was quiet and the Marconi wireless set was off. The scraps of paper and worn pencil stubs that Harold used to jot down incoming messages were scattered all over his desk and his headphones were hanging from a hook on the nearby wall.

A curtain separated Harold's bunk from the rest of the tiny office, and Olivia could hear him sleeping soundly on the other side. Although she watched the clock impatiently, she did not disturb him. She knew that this was the last good sleep he was likely to get for the next several days.

Eventually, his steady breathing sputtered into a tired yawn and she heard bones popping as he stretched awake behind the curtain. A moment later, he pulled it aside and tiredly rubbed his mess of unruly hair. He was still yawning when he looked up and saw Olivia sitting there. Startled, he yelled out and jumped so suddenly that he smacked his head on the top of the bunk with a loud metallic thud.

"Geez! Holy Moly, Olive Oil! You scared the life out of me!"

Olivia winced as Harold rubbed his injured head. "Sorry."

Harold looked around the quiet office. "What are you doing in here so early?"

"I need to talk with you about something." Olivia said. "It's important."

Harold, still rubbing the back of his head, looked at her questioningly. "Alright. What's on your mind?"

Olivia had considered very carefully how to accomplish the third task on her list, and in the end she had decided that Harold was the key. If she could get him to believe her, then it would bring them a little closer to their goal.

Olivia leveled a serious look at Harold and spoke as slowly and clearly as she could. "Tonight, at fifteen minutes past midnight, you are going to get the most important message of your life."

Harold, trying to flatten his unruly morning hair, stifled another yawn. "What are you going on about, Olive Oil?"

"The RMS Titanic is going to hit an iceberg tonight at 11:40 pm and they will start calling for help on their wireless at 12:15. The ship is going to sink, Harold. There are over two thousand people onboard and most of them are going to die."

Harold blinked at her. "Geez, Olive Oil. That's a terrible thought! Why on earth would you imagine such a thing? Did you have a bad dream or something? Is that why you're in here so early?"

Olivia shook her head. "No. Listen Harold, this is not a dream. I know this is going to happen... and the Carpathia is going to be the only ship close enough to help. Just a few years ago, if something like this had happened, then everyone aboard the Titanic would probably have died, alone, out in the middle of nowhere. Now we have wireless, though, and because of you, we will know what's happening and we'll be able to save some of them."

Harold couldn't help but smile sleepily. "Gee... that makes me feel kinda special there, Olive Oil. Thanks. Still, there's no way you could ever know that something like that is really going to happen, sweetie... and I pray for all of our sakes that it never does... especially to a big steamer like the Titanic! Sheesh! Could you imagine?"

Olivia leaned forward and handed him a slip of paper. "This will be the message you get from the Titanic tonight after midnight." she said calmly.

Harold took the note and read it aloud. "CQD. MGY. 41.46N. 50.14W." His eyes widened and his smile grew. "Wow, kiddo! That's pretty neat. How did you know those were the Titanic's call letters? And how did you know that CQD is the distress call?" He grinned at her. "I think that all the tapping you've been hearing through that wall has been soaking into your brain at night. You might be a wireless operator yet!"

"I know you don't believe me yet." Olivia continued calmly, "Which is why I'm telling you this now. I'm hoping that when the time comes, you will see that I'm telling you the truth and it will help you to make the right decision."

Harold, still smiling, looked back up at her. "The right decision? About what?"

"When the Titanic hits the iceberg, the ship's officers will only have time to do a rough estimate of their location. It's going to be off about thirteen miles." She leaned forward and handed Harold another slip of paper. "These are the actual coordinates. 41.43N 49.56W."

Harold took the paper and looked at the numbers curiously. "That must've been some detailed dream you had there, Olive Oil."

"It wasn't a dream, Harold." Olivia said once more. "And when the time comes, you are going to have to make the decision whether or not to give the captain the coordinates the Titanic sends you, or the true coordinates you're holding in your hand right now."

Harold scratched his head. His grin had faded now into just a confused curl on his lip. "I'm probably going to be asleep by 12:00 tonight anyway." he said with a shrug.

"No you won't." Olivia said as she stood up to go. "Sorry again about your head. I really didn't mean to scare you."

Harold shook his head at her with a lopsided grin. "You didn't really scare me until you started handing me these papers."

"Don't lose those." Olivia said as she moved towards the door to his office. "I'll be back tonight. I want to be here when that first call comes in."

Olivia met her father just as he was coming off shift. His face was blackened with soot and he looked exhausted, but lit up with a huge smile when he saw Olivia.

She jumped into his arms for a hug and he tried to push her away with a laugh. "I'm filthy, Peach Muffin! You don't want to get your clothes dirty."

"I don't care." Olivia said, hugging him tightly, and a moment later he pulled her up into a big bear hug in his sooty arms.

"Did you have a good night?" he asked her.

"Terrible." she said. "What about you?"

"Not too bad, actually. Curly put me on furnace number two and it was like a tropical vacation compared to my usual shift."

Olivia smiled. "That sounds nice."

Her father laughed. "Don't get me wrong. It was still back-breaking work that I wouldn't wish on my worst enemy... but overall I feel pretty good."

"That's good." Olivia said, absently wiping some of the inky blackness from his rough cheek. "Listen... try to get some good sleep today. I have a feeling it's going to be a rough night tonight."

Ben Grace looked at his daughter suspiciously. "What do you mean?"

"I just mean get some rest." Olivia insisted, then added quickly. "But don't sleep so soundly that you can't hear it if one of your bunkmates tries to sneak up on you."

Now her father looked thoroughly confused. "Sneaks up on me? Olivia Michelle Grace, what on earth are you talking about?"

Olivia forced herself to smile. "Nothing. Never mind. Just... be careful, okay?"

He looked at her for a moment longer, then kissed her cheek playfully. "You be careful, too, Peach Muffin. I love you."

"I love you, too, Daddy." Olivia smiled, then watched him as he disappeared down the ladder that led to the showers and changing rooms.

As she watched him go, she couldn't help but feel a sickening dread in her stomach that it would be the last time she would ever see him.

Chapter Twenty-four

At 12:00 noon, Olivia sat with Bubs in the teak chairs on the upper deck and watched as the captain and his officers took the noontime bearings and jotted out their calculations.

They were too far away to hear what they were saying, but to Olivia it seemed like they were taking longer than usual. In fact, after jotting down some numbers and shaking his head, the captain lifted his sextant and began taking the measurements a second time.

"Do you think Curly did his part and slowed us down?" Bubs asked anxiously as he watched the officers.

"I hope so." Olivia answered tensely.

"What are you going to do with your half of the money?" Bubs asked.

Olivia shook her head. "I don't care about the money, Bubs."

"I know." he prompted. "Still, though. You might get up to ten dollars! I don't think I've ever had that much money at one time."

They watched as the gathered officers compared notes. Eventually they must have agreed on their coordinates and they packed up and moved down the nearby stairwell as a group, led by Captain Rostron.

Olivia wanted to follow them. She couldn't stand not knowing. She knew she would have to wait until the announcement at one o'clock, though.

Bubs watched the officers go, too, and after a moment he seemed to remember something. "Oh! Hey! I almost forgot…" Bubs narrowed his eyes and looked around the empty deck cautiously. "I have what we need for our other mission today." he said, trying his best to talk without moving his lips in case someone watching could read what he was saying.

Olivia frowned at him. "What do you have? And… why are you talking like that?"

Like a spy making a secret exchange, Bubs looked around again dramatically before sliding his closed hand towards her. When Olivia just stared at him in confusion, he motioned towards his cupped hand until she lifted up her own palm and he was able to slip something into it.

She looked to see a small black disk in her hand, about half as wide as a dime and twice as thick.

"What is this?" Olivia asked.

"Magnet." Bubs responded through clenched teeth, still eyeing the empty deck around them. "My mom had a change purse with a magnetic clasp. I snuck into her things while they were on shift and I pried the magnet out." He looked around again shiftily and leaned towards her. "I stole it." He whispered meaningfully.

"Oh!" Olivia nodded, finally understanding.

"We can use it to throw off the ship's compass." Bubs explained.

Olivia looked at the tiny magnet doubtfully. "We'll have to get it right up against the compass housing for this to do anything." she said with a frown. "Even then, it might not be strong enough to do anything at all."

Bubs looked disappointed and stopped his scan of the deck for a moment. "Did you have something better?" he countered.

Olivia could see that his feelings were hurt. "No, no. This is perfect Bubs. Thank you. I know that you... um... risked a lot to get this."

That seemed to placate him. He nodded and sat back in his chair while continuing to cut his eyes around the deck.

It was all still a game to him, Olivia realized. As unnerving as this was to her, Bubs still didn't believe that a word of it was true... but it was an adventure just the same.

She sighed and slipped the magnet into her pocket. There was still a lot to do before tonight.

At one o'clock, the ship's whistle sounded to call everyone to the first class lounge for the results of the sweepstakes.

Olivia and Bubs, who were already seated in the back of the room, watched as it slowly filled up with passengers from all classes, many of them chatting and laughing excitedly. Soon the room was packed and a hush fell over the crowd as Captain Rostron and his officers stepped in.

"Good afternoon, everyone!" Captain Rostron greeted them. "I trust that you are all having a pleasant trip so far."

There was a murmur of agreement and the captain smiled. "I've been told by our Chief Purser, Mr. Brown, that the sweepstakes booty is almost as high as it has ever been! Thirty-seven dollars and twenty cents. Is that correct, Mr. Brown?"

Purser Brown, standing nearby, nodded in agreement, and excited whispers rippled thought the crowd.

The captain continued. "Most unusually, we also seem to have made less headway over the past twenty-four hours than expected."

Olivia felt her stomach clench in anticipation. Without realizing it, her lips were muttering a silent prayer.

"Our current bearings show that since noon yesterday, the Carpathia has travelled 293 miles. Putting us at a position of…"

Olivia felt like cheering. Two hundred and ninety-three miles! That was perfect! Even closer to perfect than she had ever hoped. Amazingly, Curly had come through and her plan had worked. Olivia turned her attention back on the captain, seeing the crowd was also stirring at the unexpected number.

"And so the person with the closest estimate, Mr. Brown?" the captain prompted.

Purser Brown handed the captain a ticket and Olivia felt her stomach clench, standing up from her chair and wiping her sweaty hands on her shirt.

The captain looked at the ticket and read the name out loud. "Mrs. Dianna Strevel, with a guess of 310 miles!"

Olivia froze in midstep, sure that she had heard wrong.

There was an excited squeal and a woman jumped forward. The crowd applauded as the captain shook her hand. "Congratulations, Mrs. Strevel. Follow Purser Brown here and he will make sure you get your winnings. Everyone else… be sure to play again tomorrow and have an excellent day."

The crowd began to disperse and Olivia still stood there, frozen to the spot, confused and disoriented.

"What happened?" Bubs asked her. "You were closer than that lady was. You said that your guess was 290, right? How come you didn't win?"

Olivia's head was buzzing now, still not understanding. "I have no idea. I bought a ticket and…"

"Olivia. There you are."

Olivia and Bubs turned to see Assistant Purser Glasser, looking pale and uneasy as he approached them.

"Hey dad!" Bubs said cheerfully.

Mr. Glasser smiled at Bubs, but then caught Olivia's eye and looked uncomfortably at the floor again. "Olivia... um... listen. I need to tell you. When you came to me yesterday to place your bet I... I thought your guess was way too low. I hated to see you waste your money and I wanted to give you a fighting chance, so I... I raised your number a bit."

Olivia was thunderstruck. "You *what?*"

Mr. Glasser wrung his hands. "I've been doing this for years and the distance travelled in clear weather at twelve knots is *always* higher than that. I don't understand what happened. I know that you and your father don't have much, so I was trying to help you. I didn't want you to waste your money on such an impossible number. I had no idea that..."

"We should have won!" Olivia nearly shouted.

"I know, I know." Mr. Glasser said miserably. "And I feel absolutely terrible about it, too." He reached into his pocket and pulled out a coin. "Here," he said. "This is from my own pocket to replace the one you lost because of me. I know that it's not the same as getting the winnings that you could have had, but at least you're no worse off than you were before."

He put the shiny silver dime in Olivia's hand and she just stared at it wordlessly. "I am really very, very, sorry." the assistant purser said again. Then, apparently unable to think of any more words of apology, he stepped away and left her standing alone again with Bubs.

Olivia stared down at the dime in her hand.

Two hundred and ninety-three miles! She should have been overjoyed.

Instead, though, her thoughts were filled with the enraged visage of Curly. In her mind's eye, his expression was murderous. He would think that he had been tricked. He would think that Olivia had cheated him somehow and the next time she saw him, she knew that there would be nothing to hold him back from beating her as he had always wanted to do.

Bubs was watching Olivia in uncomfortable silence. "Wow. Olivia. That's just…"

"It doesn't matter." Olivia said, trying to clear her head and focus again. "What's important is that now we'll be closer to the Titanic when the time comes. If we can throw off the compass to get us to drift a little further north, then we could be less than an hour's distance from the Titanic when she calls."

Bubs swallowed nervously. "Yeah, but what are you going to do about Curly? He's going to be…"

"It doesn't matter." Olivia said again firmly. She knew that there would be no consoling Curly and she also knew that he would more than likely take out his rage on her father… but she couldn't think about any of that now. She had set something in motion and it was too late to do anything but see it through. In less than ten hours the Titanic would strike the iceberg and right now all she could focus on was saving as many of those lives as she possibly could.

She reached into her pocket and pulled out the tiny magnet that Bubs had stolen for her.

"Let's go to the Bridge." Olivia said with quiet determination.

Bubs watched her for a long moment, perhaps realizing that this fun adventure was turning out to be much more serious than he had anticipated. Finally, he took a deep breath and followed Olivia out of the lounge.

Chapter Twenty-Five

Bubs had devised an elaborate plan for sabotaging the ship's compass. He had worked out every detail in a written script, which included him faking a heart attack to draw the attention of the officers on the bridge to give Olivia a chance to get near the compass unnoticed.

Despite the absurdity of a 10-year-old having a heart attack, Bubs was quite excited about the plan and had been practicing for most of the previous night. He showed Olivia his dramatic rendition, complete with bulging eyes, gagging noises, and unsightly drool. Even if they didn't believe it was a heart attack, it would definitely be an effective diversion.

Bubs never got the chance to put on his show, though. When they went up to the bridge around 1:30, most of the officers were off duty for lunch. There was only a young, fresh-faced junior officer manning the wheel and looking out at the open sea ahead.

Bubs looked ready to launch into his practiced heart attack anyway, but Olivia caught his arm just as he was reaching up to clutch his chest. Instead, she smiled brightly up at the young man as he turned to look at them.

"Um... you two shouldn't be up here. No passengers allowed on the bridge without..."

"We're not passengers." Olivia reassured cheerfully, stepping into the glassed-in wheelhouse and pulling Bubs behind her. "My father is a fireman and Bubs' father is Assistant Purser. We live onboard."

The junior officer didn't know quite how to respond to that. "Oh, well... uh... I'm still not sure that..."

"Aw, it's okay." Olivia smiled as she and Bubs saddled up on either side of the officer. "We just wanted to see the wheelhouse. We promise we won't touch anything."

Olivia had been able to slip up right beside the compass and now leaned against it lightly as she continued to flash a winning smile at the wary-looking young man. Bubs, on the other side of him, started to finger the engine control lever nearby. Currently, it was pushed forward to "All Ahead".

"Don't touch that!" the young officer snapped nervously, and while his attention was turned from her, Olivia pulled the tiny magnet out of her pocket and pushed it up against the side of the compass. She saw the compass needle twitch slightly, but then realized with dismay that the compass housing was made of wood and the magnet wouldn't stick to it to stay in place.

Olivia fumbled with the tiny magnet for a moment, almost dropping it, and the junior officer turned to look at her. "What are you doing? You really need to step away from..."

"Look!" Bubs shouted suddenly. "A whale!!"

The officer and Olivia both snapped their heads up to look out the window at the open sea in front of the ship. There was nothing there but rolling blue water to the horizon.

"Where?" the young officer snapped.

"He was dead ahead." Bubs said intently, pointing to nothing in particular.

Realizing that he was giving her the chance she needed, Olivia fumbled around the wooden casing frantically until she found where it was anchored to its stand with an iron bolt. She pressed the button magnet there and it stuck in place, moving the compass needle just a twitch to the left. It wasn't as much as she would've liked, but it would be enough to steer the ship a little further north than it would have been otherwise.

Bubs was watching her from the corner of his eye, and when he saw that she had successfully attached the magnet, he clicked his tongue and folded his arms across his chest. "Oops! Sorry. Just a wave, I guess. Well... I suppose we'll be going now. You've got some important... uh... steering to do and we don't want to take up any more of your time."

Olivia smiled at the confused-looking junior officer. "Drive carefully." she said, then a moment later, they made their hasty retreat.

Now that everything was in place, Olivia could do little more for the remainder of the afternoon but sit and pray.

The Titanic would still hit the iceberg at 11:40 and would still slip under the water at 2:20. Nothing she did could change those things. Hopefully, though, her efforts would make sure the Carpathia arrived on the scene sometime in between to save as many passengers as possible and... this thought still terrified Olivia beyond imagining... give her time to get aboard the sinking ship and retrieve the package for Dumas.

Eating was out of the question. Olivia was so on-edge that just the thought of food made her sick to her stomach. She spent dinnertime in her room instead, struggling to recall a sketchy map of the Titanic from her memory that could help lead her to the flooding mail room when the time came.

Tracing her steps on the yellowed scraps of paper made her realize how foolhardy and dangerous it would be to even try to do what Dumas had asked. She remembered the old woman's deadly threats, though, and realized that there was no other choice.

It was well into the evening when she crawled out of her room through the maze of pipes and stepped into Harold's office next door. He was listening to the wireless traffic on his headphones and jotting down notes on scraps of paper nearby. Olivia walked right up beside him before he realized she was there.

He pulled off his headphones. "Hey there, Olive Oil." he said with a smile, although not as cheerfully as he usually did.

"Hi, Harold." Olivia said. "Any word from the Titanic yet?"

Harold sighed, giving Olivia a sideways look. "I could hear them tapping out messages this morning, but they've been quiet now for a while. Lots of folks have been trying to reach them, though. Mostly trying to relay personal messages, but also some ice warnings and—"

"Ice warnings?" Olivia cut in.

Harold could see what she was thinking. "Yes, but they're not that unusual this time of year, Olive Oil. We've had ice warnings every crossing for months. In fact, with all of the ships passing warnings back and forth with wireless, it would be almost impossible for a ship to hit an iceberg these days."

Olivia chewed her lip thoughtfully. "The Titanic is quiet now because their wireless set is down. Bride and Phillips are working to fix it and tonight they'll be so busy trying to catch up on all of the personal messages they missed that they are going to ignore all of the ice warnings coming in."

"Jack Phillips and Harold Bride? Hey! I know those guys. I went through training with them. But how did you know they were working the Titanic?"

"I know a lot of things, Harold. You'll realize that when the time comes. I'm really counting on you."

169

It was 11:30 pm when Olivia made her way up to the top deck, wrapped warmly in an old blanket. She looked up at the clock set into the wall above the nearby stairwell, then took a deep breath and turned out to the immense darkness of the open ocean.

She had read books about soldiers preparing for a battle where they faced hopeless odds… and she realized that they must have felt something like what she was feeling herself at that moment. She wondered again why God would have chosen her for such an overwhelming task and she felt nearly helpless at the thought that so much depended on her.

"I'm doing this for you, God." she muttered into the wind. "I'm doing this because I think that it's what you want me to do. I just… I could use a little help if you can spare it."

"Help with what?" came a voice behind her that nearly made her leap out of her skin. She spun to see Bubs there, huddled up in a tattered old coat two sizes too big for him.

Olivia cleared her throat quickly. "Nothing. Just talking to… hey… isn't it past your bedtime?"

"Yup. I snuck out. My parents are asleep already." He glanced up at the nearby clock. "It's almost time, right?"

Olivia pushed down a sickening dread in her stomach and turned again to gaze out at the cold, empty black ocean that stretched endlessly in every direction. Bubs moved up to the railing and looked out with her.

"Wow." he said. "I don't think I've ever seen it so clear and calm."

It was true. Although no moon was in sight, the stars overhead seemed to blaze in the heavens from horizon to horizon. There was no wind and the water was perfectly flat and still, broken only by the wake of the Carpathia cutting through the night.

"It's what the survivors will always remember." Olivia said quietly to herself. "It was the clearest night any of them could ever remember. People don't realize, though, that when the ocean is this calm it is also much more dangerous. With no waves to break at the base of the icebergs, it makes them almost impossible to see. When the lookout, Frederick Fleet, does see something ahead and sends warning down to the bridge... it is already too late. The ship is too big and moving too fast."

Olivia swallowed and stared out at the water, as if in a trance. "It's just a shudder to most of the passengers. Just a tremble that doesn't even wake most of them up. It rattles some of the dishes in the cupboards and sends ripples through the half-empty wine glasses of the men still playing cards in the first class lounge... but to most of the thousands it just goes unnoticed. The iceberg is as big as a mountain and towers even above the highest deck of the ship as it scrapes by, shaving off big chunks of ice onto the decks before it passes them silently and disappears again into the darkness behind them. A few are up on the deck to see it pass... but most never see it at all."

Olivia looked again at the clock and realized that it was happening right then. It was happening at that very moment. The Titanic had just brushed the iceberg and its fate was sealed.

"They'll close the watertight doors." Olivia said softly. "The ones that are supposed to make her unsinkable. They can only slow down the inevitable, though. The damage is too great. Before long they will realize that the big ship is sinking and there aren't enough lifeboats for all of those families aboard. There aren't enough lifeboats by far."

Olivia squeezed her eyes shut and a tear ran down her cheek. When she looked up again, Bubs was watching her, wide-eyed.

"This is really happening, isn't it Olivia? You didn't make up any of this, did you?"

Olivia shook her head, almost heartbroken to see the look of dawning horror on Bubs' face. This was no longer a game, he realized. No make-believe adventure.

Then Bubs frowned. "So... that means that all of it is true. You... you really went into the future?"

Olivia nodded.

Bubs looked back at her shakily. "So... this is... I mean... you're really going to try to change the course of history?"

"If I can." Olivia said quietly.

Bubs looked overwhelmed. "Well, geez... that seems..."

"Impossible?" Olivia supplied.

Bubs nodded. "Sort of... yeah."

Olivia forced herself to smile. "I guess we'll see, won't we?"

Chapter Twenty-Six

On their way down to the wireless office, they met Harold coming down the opposite stairwell and Olivia let out an audible gasp when she saw him.

"Harold!" she shouted, forgetting that there were passengers sleeping in the closed-up first class cabins nearby. "What are you doing away from your office?"

Harold smiled tiredly at Bubs. "Hey Bubs. Snazzy coat." Then, still yawning, he returned his attention to Olivia. "Ease up, Olive Oil. I had to run some messages up to the bridge. I was just heading back down now to turn in for the night."

Olivia felt like shaking him. Had he not been listening to everything she had been telling him that day? "Get down there! The Titanic is going to call at any minute and you have to be ready to run to the captain."

Harold gave Bubs a "can you believe this crazy girl" look and Olivia was proud and relieved when Bubs met it with a deadly serious glare.

Seeing that he was outnumbered, Harold let himself be herded back into his office where, to Olivia's horror, she found that the big Marconi wireless set had actually been turned off.

"Harold! Why in the world is your set off?" Olivia asked, her voice verging on panic.

"I told you Olive Oil, I was just about to pack it up for the night."

"Turn it on!" Olivia demanded, nearly hysterical now. "Call up the Titanic!"

She looked at the clock above the set and saw that it was 12:02. They were sounding the ship now, seeing the damage the silent brush with the iceberg had caused. In just a few minutes, Captain Smith would be told that his ship... the largest and most expensive vessel ever built by man... would only stay afloat for about two more hours. They would begin filling the lifeboats and the first distress signals would be sent out over wireless.

Harold stood there for a moment, looking first at Bubs, then back at Olivia. "Olive Oil, sweety. You know I love you... but I can't just ring up the Titanic and ask them if they're sinking. They'll think I'm out of my mind."

"Just call them." Olivia insisted. "It won't matter what it's about. They're going to cut you off anyway. Make up something if you have to just... call them!"

Seeing that Olivia was near tears, Harold finally held up his hands. "Alright. Ease up there. Let me warm up the set and I'll give them a call. I've actually heard Cape Race trying to get in touch with them. Guess it wouldn't hurt to pass that message on."

Harold proceeded to power on the Marconi set and Olivia could barely contain her frustration as she waited for the thing to warm up. It was 12:17 when Harold was finally seated in his chair with the headset on again, working the array of dials until he found the right settings. A moment later, he began to tap out a rapid message, his finger a blur on the hammer as it clicked in the silence of the office.

Since Bubs and Olivia were leaning over him and watching intently, he whispered as he tapped so they would know what he was sending. "This is the Carpathia calling the Titanic. Respond if you are receiving."

A moment later Olivia and Bubs could hear some cracks and pops emerge from the static issuing from Harold's headphones. He listened, then murmured. "Got them. They told me to go ahead with my message."

Bubs looked at Olivia meaningfully as Harold began to tap out his reply. "Good morning, old man." He whispered as he tapped. "Do you know that there are messages for you at Cape Race?"

Harold had barely tapped out the last bit of his message before the hurried rush of cracks and pops came spilling back at him through his headphones. As he listened to them carefully, his mouth turned downward into a frown and he grabbed a pencil and started furiously jotting something down.

Olivia leaned in as Harold was writing and... although she had been expecting it... she felt a cold fear surge through her as he scrawled out the letters.

CQD... CQD... MGY.

Come at once. We have struck a berg.

CQD. Position 41.46 N 50.14 W.

When Harold's hand stopped, he stared down at the message he had just written with stunned silence. Wordlessly, his face an ashen white, he turned and looked fearfully at Olivia.

He swallowed, then as if still not quite believing it, tapped out another message. "Should I tell my captain?" he whispered as he tapped.

The response was immediate. "Yes. Quick." Harold translated softly.

Harold sat frozen for a long moment, staring at the glowing lights of the wireless set before him as if he were in a trance. An instant later, he seemed to find his resolve and pulled off his headset quickly, reaching for the message he had just scrawled out.

Olivia placed her hand on his before he could pick it up.

"Remember what I told you." Olivia whispered urgently. "Remember the papers I gave you this morning."

Harold blinked at her, then reached into his shirt pocket and retrieved the two yellowed and crumpled scraps that Olivia had handed him that morning. He unfolded the top one and stared at it, then down at the message he had just received.

"Olivia…" he said breathlessly. "How did you… how could you have possibly…"

Olivia shook her head, speaking calmly and slowly now… understanding that this was a critical moment in her venture to change the course of history. "It doesn't matter how, Harold. What matters is what you decide to do now. Those are the wrong coordinates. When you take this message to the captain, you have got to give him the coordinates I handed you this morning if we are going to have a chance at saving all of those people."

Harold looked at her with wide eyes, then at the scraps of paper in his hand. "I can't believe this is really happening." he said.

"I told you that one day you would get an important call on that set of yours." Olivia smiled gently. "This is it. The most important call anyone has ever received."

Olivia and Bubs followed as Harold raced to the bridge and handed the scrap of paper… *Olivia's* scrap of paper… to the officer on night duty. The man took one look at the message, then looked sharply up at Harold. "The Titanic? Is this real?"

Harold cut a look to Olivia and Bubs, then nodded firmly, "Yessir. I just got the message from the Titanic operator. They're going down and need immediate assistance."

That was all the officer needed to hear. Without another word, he moved to a door just off the bridge marked "Captain's Quarters". He knocked sharply once, then... without waiting for a reply, opened the door into the darkened cabin.

Harold and the officer went inside, but Olivia held back Bubs before he could follow. Captain Rostron would be asleep and might not take too well to a crowd of people barging into his cabin unannounced.

Listening at the door, Olivia heard the Captain mutter sleepily. "What's the meaning of this?"

"This message just arrived over wireless, sir. It's the Titanic. She's struck a berg and is calling for immediate assistance."

There was a moment of silence as Captain Rostron read over the message. When he spoke next, his voice was fully awake and held the tone of clear, calm command. "Mr. Dean, turn us around." he said gravely. "Start moving north towards these coordinates. I'll work out a precise course for you in a few minutes. Rouse all of the crew and have them gather in the mess for orders, but keep things quiet. Better if we don't wake the passengers now. Harold, call the Titanic and tell them that we're on our way."

"Yessir." both Harold and the officer answered together.

The officer rushed out the door past Bubs and Olivia, but the Captain called to Harold again just as he was stepping out.

"Mr. Cottam?"

The young wireless operator turned and looked back into the cabin. "Yes Captain?"

"You're sure about this?"

Harold nodded. "Yessir."

The Captain lowered his voice. "God help us."

Harold nodded once more before stepping out. "Yessir."
he agreed solemnly.

Chapter Twenty-Seven

Watching the next thirty minutes unfold made Olivia very proud to call the Carpathia her home.

Woken in the middle of the night... many of them having just come off a full day's shift... the crew of the Carpathia gathered silently in the mess hall to await the Captain's orders. Although many looked bewildered at the midnight rousing, none of them complained. They trusted Captain Rostron and they knew that something important must be happening for him to call them all together at such an odd time.

Everyone came. Cooks and stewards, doctors and pursers, entertainers, cleaning staff... even Curly Reynolds, covered in soot, had crawled out from the bowels of the ship to answer the Captain's midnight summons.

When Olivia saw Curly, standing like a blackened and burned goblin in the doorway on the opposite side of the room, she positioned herself so that she was sure he wouldn't catch sight of her. She knew he was probably still out for her blood and… even in this time of crisis and in front of all of these people… who knew what Curly Reynolds would do if he spotted her?

When Captain Rostron stepped into the room a few minutes later, the quiet and questioning murmurs that had been rippling through the room were hushed to a dead silence.

The Captain looked fully awake and alert. No one could have ever guessed that he had been roused from a sound sleep less than ten minutes earlier. He stepped up to the front of the assembled crew and looked every bit like a general preparing to marshal his troops into battle.

"Just a few minutes ago, our wireless operator, Mr. Cottam, received a message from a nearby ship in distress. It appears that the RMS Titanic has struck ice and is floundering. She's called for help from anyone nearby and we're answering her call."

There was a shocked ripple of murmurs that ran through the gathered crowd, which fell off again to immediate silence as the captain continued.

"Now at our full cruising speed of 12 knots, I put us to be about an hour away." (*At the words, Olivia felt an elated burst of joy and dizzying fear. She had accomplished the impossible!*)

Rostron turned to the blackened form of Curly then. "We don't know how fast she's going down and every minute counts. Mr. Reynolds, I want every stoker on duty feeding those furnaces. Cut the hot water and heat off from the rest of the ship and pour every ounce of steam into getting us moving as fast as we can."

Curly nodded his misshapen head and muttered "Yes, Cap'n" before disappearing to carry out his orders.

Rostron continued a list of orders and preparations then, turning to various other crew members as he assigned each task. "I want extra lookouts posted on all points. In the nests and on the bow. We've got to move fast, but there've been reports of ice pouring in from all over this area. Bergs, growlers, and pack ice. If it can take down a ship as big as the Titanic, then it's all the more dangerous for us."

"We need to get these new passengers safely onboard, and we need to be ready for anything. Have all lifeboats prepped and swung out. Ready nets and ladders at all cargo and gangway doors and string electric lights along all sides of the ship so we can see survivors in the water and hoist them up. Have some burlap bags tied with rope so we can pull up any small children who can't climb. Klimczak, have your men prepare oil bags to pour on the ocean in case the water gets rough."

"Dr. Blackmarr—have your staff setup medical stations in the dining halls in first, second, and third classes. Purser's Brown and Glasser—I want you and your staff at every entrance recording the name and class of every man, woman, and child brought aboard. Chief Cook Stevenson—have the mess crew in every class begin preparing hot coffee, tea, and soup. It's below freezing out there and we're going to have to warm these people up when they come aboard."

"Stewards— bring any extra blankets and linens to the medical stations the doctors are setting up and I want all of the empty rooms prepped to take on passengers. Down in steerage, move the passengers to double-up in all quarters. Eight to a room. I want the same with the crew quarters. The Titanic is a big ship. With all of her passengers and crew, we could be looking at over three thousand coming aboard and we need to make space for them."

There was another startled ripple through the crowd as that immense number settled in and Rostron, having issued all of his orders, paused for a moment to look out over the room.

"Let's keep things as quiet as we can." He added solemnly. "Things are going to get stirred up enough around here without our own passengers panicking and getting in the way. If they wake up, try to keep them in their staterooms and tell them to remain there until they hear otherwise." Rostron took a deep breath, pausing for a moment to look around the room before finishing with a decisive nod. "You all have your orders. Let's get them done."

The crowd broke at once, everyone moving with an assigned purpose and sense of urgency. In a few moments, the mess hall was cleared and the sounds of the cook staff working frantically in the kitchens were all that broke the silence. Bubs turned to Olivia, wide-eyed and speechless.

Finally, he swallowed. "He said we were less than an hour away, Olivia. We're going to get there before they go under. You... you did it!"

"*We* did it Bubs... but don't start celebrating yet. The hard part is yet to come."

They joined the lookouts on the bow of the ship, scanning the blackness ahead for ice.

Curly had done his part down below and the Carpathia was cutting through the night faster than she had ever moved. She imagined her father down there with every other stoker onboard, frantically shoveling coal to push the Carpathia's engines beyond their limits. The massive iron hull thrummed and rattled beneath them as Bubs and Olivia squinted out at the calm, flat sea ahead with the icy headwind stinging their cheeks.

It was cold... so much colder now than it had ever been on their crossings... and Olivia knew it was because they were further north than they should have been. The magnet on the bridge compass had done its job.

"Iceberg dead ahead!" came a sudden cry from the port side and from up in the crow's nest above, a bell sounded. Orders were barked from the bridge and the massive ship lurched as she swung around hard to aft. Olivia turned just in time to see the shadow of a looming mountain passing dangerously close by. It was nearly invisible in the moonless darkness, but as it passed it gleamed icy white against the burning electric lights of the Carpathia.

While the passing berg held the attention of Olivia and several of the others on deck, Bubs nearly made her jump out of her skin when he suddenly yelled out "Lookout! There's another one! Coming up on aft!"

Seconds later, the bell in the crow's nest rung out again, followed by a call of "Iceberg aft ahead!"

The nose of the big ship swung around again and this time another looming mountain of ice passed them on the opposite side.

Olivia watched it pass, shimmering ghostly white in the glow of the ship, then turned solemnly to Bubs. "Good call, Bubs." she said.

Bubs kept his eyes forward into the wind, scanning the darkness ahead, but before she turned away, Olivia caught a twitch of a proud smile curl the edges of his lips.

It was 12:47 when they saw the first white rocket explode silently in the distance. They had all been scanning the inky blackness for the dimmest hint of ice, so when the bright light flared up suddenly it made them all jump.

It looked close... but Olivia knew that may have been a trick of the remarkably clear night. Calls were sounded from the lookouts to the bridge and the bow swung around towards the place where the white flash had lit up the horizon a moment before.

When a second rocket flared out of the night moments later, the knots in Olivia's stomach clenched so tightly that she almost felt sick. Behind her, the steam wenches that controlled the lifeboat cranes began to squeal and churn as the unpacked lifeboats were swung out over the sides. On the captain's orders, a bright green rocket was launched from the upper boat deck. It sizzled up into the starry sky and burst into a spectacular bloom of green embers above them.

Hopefully the Titanic would get the message: *help is on the way.*

Chapter Twenty-Eight

At 12:53, they could see the Titanic.

Despite how tantalizingly close the rockets had appeared, there had been no sign of the ship before then. They dodged another mountainous iceberg... pulling hard to stern then back again... and as they came around, there it was... no more than three miles out.

At first it looked as if everything were fine. The enormous liner... so impossibly long and bigger than Olivia could have imagined... was lit up brightly and sitting upright in the water. It wasn't moving, but in the silent distance, all looked peaceful... much like the captain had just decided to stop for the night.

But then, looking closer, Olivia could see that the big ship was low in the water... so much lower than it ever should have been... and (it may have been a trick of the light from this distance) the back end seemed just a little higher than the front.

When another white rocket shot into the air from the distant ship, they could see lifeboats in the water around her... reflected in the shimmering light before all went dark again.

Almost immediately, another green rocket soared into the sky and burst above the Carpathia. Olivia could only imagine what a sight they must have made, steaming over the horizon at full speed awash in the glow of their bright electric lights. She thought of the passengers standing on the deck of the Titanic... passengers that had been doomed but now saw their saviors rushing towards them from the darkness. This was it, she realized. In that moment, Olivia knew that she had irreversibly altered the course of human history. That small part of her that had still been uncertain about paradoxes and destroying the universe made her cringe for just an instant... but when the moment passed the icy wind was still stinging her cheeks and they were still cutting through the water ever nearer to the immense doomed ocean liner in the distance. The universe, despite its altered course, had remained whole and intact.

A bright light soon began flashing near the stern of the Titanic, still several miles out. On the bridge above Olivia, Captain Rostron and his officers already had their own Morse Lamp readied to reply.

"Captain Smith says that he's glad to see us, sir." one of the officers relayed to Rostron. "He says that they have a hundred and fifty in the lifeboats and two-thousand one-hundred still aboard."

"He's low in the water, but it looks like he's leveled out." Rostron commented. "Ask him what our time is."

Olivia could hear the clicking of the shutter opening and closing rhythmically as the officer flashed out Rostron's message. The response came a few moments later from the Titanic, but Olivia already knew the answer.

"They're taking on water fast, sir. One hour. His engineers estimate they can stay afloat one more hour."

Rostron said nothing, but Olivia turned to look up at him standing at the railing on the deck above and she could see his visage turn stony. She knew what he was thinking: Not enough time. That wasn't enough time by far to get that many people aboard.

It's better than what you had. Olivia thought solemnly. *Let's put it to good use.*

Finally, Rostron spoke again. "Relay to Captain Smith that we will approach as close as we dare... absolutely no closer than a thousand yards. We'll launch our lifeboats and prepare to take on theirs. Between their boats and ours, we should be able to ferry most of them across in that time."

Olivia knew that he didn't really believe that... but as Captain it was his job to put on a good face for the others.

As the officer relayed the captain's message, Olivia looked back over her shoulder at the lifeboats being readied there. Feeling a lump rise in her throat, she realized what she had to do.

Before her fear completely paralyzed her, she forced herself to move silently towards the closest lifeboat while all eyes remained fixed on the distant Titanic. Even Bubs, standing by her side, never noticed her disappearance. She crept into the boat and slipped under one of the seats and into a storage compartment there. She found a stack of life vests in the darkness and was able to slip one on silently as she hunkered down. The vest smelled of salt and wet corkwood, and even in the shelter of the storage compartment the icy air was biting at her bare hands and face.

Before long, Olivia could hear someone shouting. "Man the boats! Four men on the oars and an officer at the rudder. We've got to move like death is on our heels, boys."

There was the stomping of boots on wood and the boat she was in swayed precariously. Then, she could hear the sound of the wenches starting up and she almost let out a startled scream when the boat lurched downwards suddenly. Moments later, it hit the water and without missing a beat, someone called out "Pull!", then she heard oars splashing into the water as the boat plunged forward.

From her hiding place under the seat, Olivia couldn't see how close they were getting to the big ship, but to her it seemed to take way too long to get there. She wondered again how they could possibly hope to ferry two thousand passengers over this distance before the hour was up.

At one point, she heard the officer on her boat call out "Ahoy! What's your load?"

A man's voice, a little further away, answered the call. "We're carrying twenty-one. Eight women, ten men, and three crew."

The officer on Olivia's lifeboat sputtered back. "Twenty-one? Have you lost your mind? That boat you're in could carry almost seventy! Your captain signaled that you had over two thousand on board! How could you have launched a boat that's not even half full?"

The crewman on the other lifeboat was obviously not pleased at being chastised by someone from another ship. "I was just following orders! Take it up with Lightroller if you want to make something of it."

Then the lifeboats must have passed out of shouting range, because once again there was only silence and the steady rhythm of the oars. A moment later, though, she heard someone mutter under his breath. "Twenty-one! I hope Captain Rostron refuses to even let them aboard until they go back and fill up that boat all the way!"

The rowing must have been hard. For a long time after they had passed the other boat, the only sounds that broke the silence were the grunts and laborious breathing of the men around her, punctuated by the rhythmic splashing of the oars in the icy sea. It was maybe ten more minutes before Olivia could hear anything else again. Voices... distant at first but getting nearer. The sounds of shouted orders and rigging being worked. Something else, too. Music. A string quartet playing jaunty, upbeat music... and above it all, a distant, high-pitched screeching sound that she didn't recognize.

Olivia chanced a peek out from her hiding place and her breath caught in her throat when she saw that they were right up against the enormous bulkhead of the Titanic. Every electric light onboard was burning brightly, and passengers lined the decks, not looking the least bit panicked. In fact, some of them looked rather amused and she saw one or two actually looking down at their arriving lifeboat and waving playfully as if it had just arrived to take them for a leisurely excursion.

Looking over the railing from one of the decks far above them, one well-dressed woman stood with her husband... an older gentleman with a white handlebar mustache holding a glass of wine in one hand and a cigar in the other.

"What ship are you from?" the woman called down to the officer steering the lifeboat. Olivia noticed that she had a luxurious white fur coat draped over her shoulders and her life vest was slung carelessly over the railing beside her.

"The Carpathia, mam." the officer replied as he worked to steer the lifeboat into the rigging that could lift them up.

"The Carpathia? Isn't that a Cunard ship? Ungh, what are the first class accommodations like?"

The officer seemed a bit annoyed by the question. "Well, mam. They're a lot dryer than the rooms on the Titanic will be in an hour."

The woman seemed not to notice the sarcasm and turned to her husband. "Perhaps we should wait for the next ship. I

189

heard that the Olympic is on the way. They're supposed to have an excellent chef."

Olivia knew that the Olympic, Titanic's sister ship, was actually hundreds of miles away and wouldn't arrive until later tomorrow. She resisted the urge to stick her head out of her hiding place and shout at the woman "Don't be a fool! Just get in a boat and be happy that you're going to live to see the sun come up!"

The oarsmen who had rowed them over finished securing the rigging and there was another stomach-twisting lurch as her lifeboat was lifted out of the water and up along the side of the ship. Olivia was reminded of the glass elevator that she had ridden at HistCorp. She watched deck after deck pass by as they rose up and up and up until they finally reached the boat deck high above.

There was still little sign of panic or distress up here. In fact, there was hardly even anybody waiting to step into the lifeboats other than a few huddled families... many of whom had brought their luggage and all of their belongings up with them. The Titanic's officers were trying to call people over, urging them to get into a boat... but mostly their calls went unheard.

Olivia knew that many of the people here simply did not believe that there was any danger. They had all been convinced by the relentless press that the mighty Titanic was "unsinkable" and... like the woman who had called down to their lifeboat... most of them believed that other ships would soon arrive and there would be plenty of time to choose one that suited them (maybe even when the sun came up and it was warmer).

Olivia felt like screaming at them all. Soon, in less than an hour's time, the list of the great ship would worsen as the bow began to slip under. When that happened, the officers would no longer be struggling to convince passerbys to please get into a boat. They would be fighting the mobs of people who were pushing and shoving, desperate to get into one. Why couldn't they see that they had to get off now? There would be no other ships coming to their rescue and soon the Titanic, which seemed so safe and solid with all of its electric lights blazing and the band playing... would all be gone beneath the icy water.

When the lifeboat was finally secured in place, the men from the Carpathia greeted the Titanic's crewmen and Olivia took the opportunity to slip from her hiding place and onto the deck. As she moved into the crowd, she looked around to get her bearings.

Peering through a nearby window, she saw a fitness room. Astonishingly, the fitness instructor was inside leisurely showing several interested passengers how some of the new exercise machines worked. As one young man awkwardly tried to row on the rowing machine, a group of his friends laughed and cheered, oblivious to the mortal danger that they would soon be facing.

It all made Olivia furious, but when she saw the brass clock set into the wall behind them, she was reminded of why she was here and she bit back her welling frustration.

She turned and forced herself to keep moving. She had to trust the officers and crew to get these people moved to safety. She had her own mission to see to, and even if no one else seemed to realize the danger they were in, Olivia understood all too well that the final demise of the Titanic was fast approaching.

It was 1:21 am.

Chapter Twenty-Nine

Back on the Carpathia, the engines had been stopped and the boiler room was once again feeding the furnaces to supply hot water and heat to the staterooms above. As Ben Grace worked alongside the other stokers to rake the hot coals and keep the fires burning, a bell rang above the din and Curly Reynolds stopped shouting orders long enough to pick up a phone nearby.

He pushed one meaty, blackened hand over his other ear as he leaned into the earpiece, then mumbled an affirmative before hanging it up.

"Listen up, boys!" he boomed over the chaos. "Captain says the first boats are coming over from the Titanic and he wants to relieve their rowers for the trip back to pick up some more passengers. Johnson, Rudolph, Spina: You stay here and keep the fires hot. The rest of ya... double-time it up to deck three portside."

Although unexpected, there was no hesitation among the men as they hurried out of the boiler room. Many of them pulled off their heavy leather gloves and work hats, but Ben Grace decided to keep them on since he had an idea it may be cold out. Although he was not a seaman and had never rowed a boat before, he couldn't help but feel an excited thrill at the idea of helping in a real rescue operation. He smiled to himself and thought: I'll finally have an exciting story to tell Olivia.

From her time in the New York Public Library over a hundred years in the future, Olivia vaguely remembered that the mail room on the Titanic was near the front of the ship on the starboard side. She knew all too well from her time aboard the Carpathia, though, that the inner corridors and stairwells of a steamer were a baffling maze full of dead-ends and wrong-way turns. She stayed on the upper deck for almost the entire length of the giant ship, then found a forward starboard stairwell and took a chance that it was the one she needed.

Almost immediately, Olivia encountered a young crewman coming up the stairs the opposite way. He took one look at Olivia and grabbed her by the life vest and started dragging her with him back up to the boat deck. "Lifeboats are this way, sweetheart" he said as he pulled her along. "Come on, now. I'll show you the way."

Olivia struggled to pull from his grasp. "My parents are down in their cabin." she lied quickly. "I need to get them so they can get in a boat, too."

The crewman still dragged her along, ignoring her pleas and glancing down the other corridors looking for more stragglers as he walked. "The stewards have checked all the cabins below. Your parents are probably already on the deck looking for you. Come along now, quit wiggling. There's heavy flooding down this way. You need to stay up here and get to a lifeboat. It's women and children first."

Unable to pull free, Olivia allowed herself to be dragged all the way back up to the deck she had just come down from, and she couldn't help but feel near-panicked when she saw that almost five minutes had passed and she was now right back where she had started.

The high-pitch screeching noise that had filled the air before seemed to have doubled in volume now... and if her father had been there, he could have told her that it was the sound of steam escaping the vents as the boiler fires far down below were being extinguished by rising seawater.

The crewman had to shout to be heard over it. "Back this way." he called, dragging her towards the closest lifeboat station.

Afraid that she was about to be forcibly dumped in a lifeboat and ferried back to the Carpathia empty-handed, Olivia struggled again to pull free, then finally threw her hands up and yelled "There they are!"

The crewman turned to her questioningly.

"My parents!" Olivia shouted over the piercing wail. "I saw them over by the lifeboats on the port side."

"You sure it was them?" the crewman asked.

"Positive. Let me go so I can try to catch them and we can all get into the next boat together. They're probably worried sick about me!"

The crewman nodded and smiled to her. "Alright, sweetie. Go on. Tell your parents to get right on the next lifeboat. They shouldn't wait around, do you understand me?"

That's good advice. Olivia thought. *I wish you would explain that to everyone else around here, too...*

She smiled her best grateful-little-girl smile and started towards the port side of the ship. After a couple of steps, she chanced a look back and saw that the crewman had moved aft towards the other lifeboat stations. When she was sure he wouldn't see her, she made a break for the stairwell again.

Ben Grace arrived just in time to see the first of the Titanic passengers coming aboard.

As they stepped out of the lifeboat, passengers and crew alike looked shell-shocked and near-frozen. Ben saw that some of the men wore tuxedos and others wore bedclothes and slippers. One woman stepped off in only her nightgown, barefooted and blue in the face from the bitter cold. She was immediately attended by a host of waiting Samaritans that wrapped her in blankets and put a cup of hot coffee in her shaking hands.

One of the Carpathia's officers looked astonished as the last passengers stepped off... two shivering show dogs that were immediately wrapped in warm blankets as well.

"Is that all you got?" the older officer barked to the exhausted-looking Titanic crewman. "Where's the rest of them?"

"That's all we could fit." the Titanic crewman snapped defensively as he snatched a cup of hot coffee and gulped it down.

The Carpathia officer looked at the two dogs in disgust. "You could have fit fifty more women and children in this boat! And two more on top of that if you had left them dogs!"

The silver-haired woman who was obviously the dogs' owner gasped in shock and led her dogs away towards the medical station in the mess hall where the others from the boat were being led.

The Titanic crewman slipped past and disappeared with them, apparently having no intention of rowing back to the sinking ship to help the thousands of passengers still over there.

The Carpathia officer looked furious, but then stepped into the boat and motioned for Ben and some of the other men to follow.

"Come on, men." he said. "They were nice enough to paddle over twenty-one plus two dogs. Let's go and get the two thousand or so still left onboard before it's too late…"

Olivia moved as fast as she dared down the wooden stairs that led to the second class forward cabins. She had gone down four flights and then saw that the next landing was already awash with rising water. Hoping that she had gone down far enough, she pulled open the nearest door and ran into a corridor.

The mailroom wouldn't be in any of the passenger areas… she thought quickly, and scanned the rows of cabin doors until she came to a plain wooden door simply marked "Crew Only". She pulled open the door and found herself in what looked like a massive laundry room. It was empty and looked like it had been deserted quickly.

On one wooden table nearby, a hot iron that had been used to press the linens had been left lying on a white sheet and was burning a smoking black hole into it. Olivia lifted the iron and tossed it into a nearby washbasin full of soapy water. "I've got enough to worry about without having to deal with the ship catching on fire." she mumbled.

There were two doors leading out from the laundry and Olivia picked one and ran through it, feeling her time ticking away quickly. She found herself in a crew service corridor and this one had some signs posted. Purser's offices, infirmary, wireless… all pointing in different directions. She decided to head towards the purser and at the next intersection, she was rewarded with a small stenciled sign that said "Mail Sorting" and pointed to the right. She took off down the corridor at a full run.

At the end of the corridor was a stairwell leading downward, and when Olivia looked down, she saw a door on the landing below halfway submerged in water. The black lettering on the door read "Mail Sorting room—upper level."

Olivia looked at the water and hesitated, but she knew that if she waited too long, any chance she had at getting Dumas' package would be gone. Bracing herself, she leapt down the last few stairs and splashed into the water.

Immediately, Olivia screamed.

Jumping into the icy water was like being stabbed with a million tiny icicles all over her lower body. The water came up to her stomach, and immediately her legs were in such numbing agony that for a long moment she struggled to even move them to get to the door. The pain was nearly unbearable.

As she lost the feeling in her frozen legs, she yelled out and lunged forward, falling into the door and frantically grabbing for the latch. She managed to fumble it open and a moment later a rush of water and mail surged out against her, filling the flooded stairwell landing with a sea of floating envelopes and papers carried upon the icy current.

Using her arms, Olivia pulled herself through the door and into the flooded sorting room. She found herself on the upper landing of a large room that was completely submerged under water. Even though it was flooded, the electric lights down below somehow still burned brightly, causing blurred rippling shadows to reflect up against the walls and ceiling.

Mail was everywhere. Loose letters floated and swam both on the surface of the water and down below, and waterlogged packages and parcels drifted and bumped against one another as they swam in the swirling currents.

I'm too late. Olivia thought, dismayed, as she looked at the submerged mailroom down below. She stared hopelessly at the chaotic torrent of water and mail, then let out a startled cry when she saw movement across the landing amid the floating debris.

There was a man there. With his back turned, Olivia could only see a shock of wild white hair as he struggled to stand in the waist-deep water and lift a huge mailbag onto the highest shelves. It was the last dry place in the room, and Olivia saw that he had managed to shove so many of the massive bags onto the shelf that they now were on the verge of toppling down and crushing him beneath their weight.

"No no no!" he was muttering frantically to himself. "The mail! Why haven't they come to save the mail? We've got to get these to the lifeboats! This won't do! This won't do!"

"Hey!" Olivia yelled out over the rush of water… and her voice echoed oddly in the half-submerged mailroom. "Sir! Can you please help me? I need to find something!"

The man jumped and spun around towards Olivia. She saw now that his glasses were hanging lopsided off his face and his skin and lips had turned blue from being in the freezing water for so long.

"Who are you?" the man snapped warily, squinting half-blind at her. "Have you come to help save the mail?"

"I need to find a package." Olivia yelled out through trembling lips. The numbness in her legs was creeping up her waist now. She felt like her whole body was turning to ice.

"We've got to get these bags to the lifeboats!" the man yelled out. "This is the mail! We're charged with carrying the mail! We can't let it get wet like this! We can't…"

Then, as Olivia watched in horror, the mailbags that the man had stacked into a precarious mountain above his head suddenly tipped forward and toppled in an avalanche over him. Olivia screamed, but even as she struggled to make her way there, the bags continued to fall, burying the man under the icy water with hundreds of pounds of parcels on top of him.

Olivia grabbed onto the pipes running along the ceiling and pulled herself hand-over-hand as quickly as she could toward the buried man. She threw herself onto the burlap bags and began pulling at them, throwing them back behind her into the rising water. She felt hot tears stinging her eyes and was vaguely aware that she was sobbing, but as she pulled off bag after bag, she began to realize that it had already been too long. The man was dead.

Chapter Thirty

Even with the water rising quickly in the room and the icy cold stabbing at her skin, Olivia at that moment forgot all about the danger her own life was in and was overwhelmed by the loss of the old man.

She stood there for a moment, dazed and stunned, feeling again so powerless to face the chaos unfolding around her.

Then, her eyes focused on the mailbag she was holding in her hands. She had tossed the others aside and there were still many more piled below, but the one bag she held onto had the word "Boston" stamped in ink across its white canvas.

Olivia blinked at the bag and, realizing that it was too much to hope for, pulled open the drawstring top and plunged her arm inside.

She pulled out handfuls of letters... papers of all shapes and sizes. There were rolled-up parchments and lacy white envelopes. She tossed them carelessly into the rising water around her and plunged back in for more.

Her searching fingers finally brushed something more sizeable... a parcel... and she dug it out quickly.

It was a small box wrapped in red wax paper. The address was to Mrs. Sylvia Miller.

She threw it aside, starting to feel real panic as the room closed in and the water continued to rise. It was only two feet from the ceiling now and Olivia was struggling to stay afloat. She looked across at the open hatch that led to the stairwell. She should make a break for it now. She was going to be trapped and die here in the icy water like the old man...

Instead of leaving, she plunged her arm again into the sinking mailbag. More letters, papers, another parcel... still not the right one.

The water seemed to be rising more quickly now.

It was so cold. Olivia struggled to maintain her grip on the mailbag, but found that the fingers of her left hand were too numb to hold on. Strangely, her right hand, which had been numb for days since she had returned, seemed unaffected by the cold.

The bag was still half full. She would have to abandon this. Whatever it was that Dumas had wanted, it would go to the bottom of the ocean just as it was meant to.

Still, she gritted her teeth and plunged her arm into the bag one more time. There were some more parcels down near the bottom. Her numb and icy fingers brushed them. She grabbed one frantically and pulled it out.

A small brown paper-wrapped parcel. It was already wet, but even with the ink blurred and smeared across the paper, Olivia could see clearly that it was addressed to Mr. Clive Arogia of 31 Poplar Drive, Boston.

This was it.

Olivia could barely move now. The water was rushing into the room from somewhere and the strong current was trying to pull her under.

She stuffed the package into her vest and, with trembling hands, she reached above herself to grab onto the pipes along the ceiling. Her left hand wouldn't even close anymore, but she was able to get a grip with her right hand and she started to pull towards the door.

She had just begun to move when suddenly a bony hand shot up out of the water and grabbed her wrist.

Olivia looked down and saw the frozen blue fingers gripping her and seconds later the puffy blue face of the old man broke the surface of the water. His wild tangle of white hair was matted against his skull and his blue eyes, which had seemed dazed and unfocused before, were now locked onto her with a severe intensity.

"Olivia!" the old man croaked in an icy voice that echoed in the shrinking space between the rising water and the ceiling.

This time, Olivia screamed. She screamed and kicked and fought to break free of the old man's grasp with a blind terror that blotted out all other thoughts.

"Olivia!" the old man choked again, and Olivia knew that this corpse had no right to know her name. This had to be a dream. She was dead already... drowned in the icy water... and this was a dream.

"Olivia! Listen! It's me... Chuck!"

Olivia, still caught in the grip of her panic, almost didn't hear him. It took her another few seconds to stop screaming and look again into the old man's eyes... although her heart continued to race furiously.

His icy grip on her arm was real. This was no dream.

"What?" she choked, her head spinning in confusion at the corpse's words.

"It's Chuck. Chuck Ferryman. Remember me?"

Olivia blinked at the horrifying blue face of the old man she had just watched die. "H... how? That's impossible..."

The old man snorted. "Weren't you the one always telling me that nothing is impossible?"

Olivia was trembling uncontrollably. The water was up to her neck now.

202

The old man's blue eyes darted towards the door on the other side of the room, which was now completely submerged.

"Listen... we don't have much time. I needed to tell you... you cannot let that package get in the hands of Dumas. We're fighting her, Olivia. A group of us who are brave enough to stand up to her... we've started something like our own rebel alliance against her evil empire. She's corrupted... and if she gets hold of what's in that package, she'll be almost unstoppable."

"But my father..." Olivia stammered. "She threatened to..."

The water rose above Olivia's mouth and she gagged and struggled to breathe.

"Go!" the old man rasped. "Get to a lifeboat! Don't give her that package! It's all up to you, Olivia. So much is depending on you!"

Then the water was up to the ceiling and Olivia was blinded by icy daggers stabbing at her eyes.

She felt hands upon her and suddenly she was being pushed through the water. Her shoulder hit something hard and spun her out of the grasp of the bony fingers, but she was caught in a fast current now, rushing down flooded corridors and being thrown head over heels with a rush of other debris: chairs, tables, papers and linens. She ricocheted from the metal walls, trying desperately to cover her head. Her lungs burned for air, but worst of all was the cold, which seemed to set her whole body on fire.

Her air was running out and white bursts were popping in her head as she fought to find the surface to get a breath. As she buffeted in the torrent, she flailed about until her fingers miraculously latched onto something solid.

She pulled hard and her head broke the surface of the water again. Gagging and choking, she pulled air into her lungs while struggling to hold on to the railing she had found... knowing that if she was pulled back into the current that she would never find air again.

She was at the base of a stairwell and the water was rising fast.

When she looked up, she saw that the door above her was open to the boat deck outside.

Chapter Thirty-One

The upper decks were chaos.

Olivia dragged herself, numb and trembling, out into the open air. She had the package pushed safely into her life vest, but her frozen legs couldn't even support her and she had to crawl out onto the deck with the water still rising up the stairwell at her heels.

The passengers, so calm and disinterested before, now scrambled in every direction, shouting and weeping and calling for loved ones over the din. Olivia saw one group of older gentlemen standing on the first class promenade above her. They were all dressed in dapper dinner jackets and were standing calmly together, watching the scene around them.

Amazingly, she still heard music playing... a sad, sorrowful melody that drifted up into the night above all of the other sounds.

The massive ship was tilted at a frightening angle. The whole bow, just forward of the stairwell that Olivia had emerged from, was completely underwater. The icy black ocean spilled out onto the deck and over the railing that had just an hour before been almost sixty feet above the surface. Olivia's gaze moved up the incline towards the back of the ship, which rose out of the water and into the sky with its bright electric lights still gleaming in the darkness.

Most of the passengers had retreated there now, but many were still trying for the lifeboats as well. She saw crew—both from the Titanic and the Carpathia—trying to pack lifeboats nearby as mobs of people pushed for a space. There were so many people (*too many*, Olivia realized) still aboard. She had hoped that by now most of the passengers would have been safely away. They had been too slow to realize the danger, though. Now, for many of them, it would be too late.

The lifeboat closest to Olivia, on the aft side of the ship, was already so packed that its sides floated only inches out of the water. As they rowed away, Olivia saw that one of the people rowing was a finely dressed young woman with her red hair done up in an elegant bun. She pulled at the oars just as skillfully as the burly men rowing beside her.

Olivia's eyes wouldn't focus and she had to rub away the stinging pain to try and get her bearings. She was out of the water for the moment, but it was rising fast and if she didn't start moving again, she would be swept off the deck. The air, though not as brutally cold as the icy water had been, was still frigid.

There was a flash of green as a flare climbed into the night sky and Olivia turned to see the Carpathia floating in the distance, lights ablaze in the darkness. Between them was a line of lifeboats on the black water… some coming and some going. There were swimmers, too… some people who thought they could somehow make it out to the Carpathia even though she was a thousand yards away through the icy water.

Olivia struggled to pull herself up the slope of the deck ahead of the rising water at her heels. She passed the gym again and was horrified to see that the clock on the back wall now read 2:16.

Olivia's mind struggled to remember the timeline of events that she had memorized. The ship would be gone at 2:20... plunging miles to the bottom of the ocean. It would all begin to happen very fast now.

In that moment, as if to confirm Olivia's fears, the lights went out.

In the sudden darkness, everyone around her seemed to quiet for a moment and hold their breath. A chilling hush fell over the whole scene. Then the lights came back on and began to burn so brightly that they made Olivia squint. A light bulb in the gymnasium shattered with explosive force, then the ship was plunged completely into darkness again... this time for good.

An instant later, the screaming began again.

The lights of the Carpathia could still be seen gleaming in the close distance, giving off the only light in the blackness. They seemed so near but still painfully out of reach.

Even as her mind raced, struggling to decide her next move, Olivia heard a shuddering tearing of metal... a sound that roared out into the night like a monstrous peel of thunder. She looked back to see one of the towering funnels ripping free at its base. As tall as a city building, the tremendous steel structure fell forward in slow motion.

Olivia, like the others around her, watched in stricken horror as the funnel fell towards the swimmers in the water and the approaching lifeboats.

Ben Grace had made one crossing already, pulling with all of his strength on the oars to carry the Titanic's passengers to the safety of Carpathia.

There had been a group of men ready to take his place for a second trip back, but Ben had opted to stay. He had seen the relieved expressions of the men, women, and children as they were raised up to safety and it had given him a sense of accomplishment unlike any he had ever felt in his hours of stoking the fires. He had helped saved these people's lives, he realized… and he wanted to save more.

Rowing back to the Titanic for the second trip was a much different venture, though.

The bright electric lights on the long ocean liner still burned brightly in the icy darkness, but now everyone could see that the end was coming fast. The front of the great ship was almost entirely underwater… and the stern was actually lifted into the air above the surface, exposing part of the tremendous three-story high propellers. It was a terrible, mesmerizing thing to see.

The ocean between the Titanic and the Carpathia was chaotic. Besides watching for other lifeboats, the men rowing had to also be careful of the swimmers in the water. Several times they would stop and pull a half-frozen passenger aboard. Sometimes they had been holding on to a deck chair or other piece of floating debris, but Ben helped pull one woman onboard who had swum almost the entire distance without even a life vest. Other times, they would pull alongside a person and realize that they were too late to save them. They hated to leave these lifeless bodies in the water, but they knew that they needed every available space for those they could save.

All of this made it slow going and by the time they were within a hundred yards of the Titanic again, their boat was already half full.

They had to move fast, they knew. Captain Rostron had given them strict orders to get clear of the big ship once it started going down fast. Nobody had ever seen a ship this size sink, and he was afraid that the suction of the steel giant going under would pull with it everything nearby.

As they approached, they found the currents near the sinking bow were already strong, and the men rowing had to struggle to keep the lifeboat straight. The wake of the big ship slipping under was already too much to fight.

By now, many of the passengers still on the Titanic had spotted their boat and some had jumped into the water to try and swim to them. Ben pulled hard at the oars with the other men and broke them free of a strong current, but many of the swimmers found themselves trapped and unable to escape themselves.

Ben saw a young woman in the water struggling to swim with a small boy clinging to her shoulders. As he watched, they were pulled under. When the boy broke the surface again, he was alone clinging only to an empty life vest and caught helplessly in the icy current.

Without thinking, Ben threw down his oar and dove in after him.

The water was unimaginably cold, and pain seared through his entire body. The current seemed to work in his favor and when it shifted, the screaming boy surged right into his grasp and immediately latched on to him... but now Ben was fighting to stay afloat himself. The water spun him and he lost sight of the lifeboat.

As he turned, he caught sight of a girl on the deck of the Titanic. She was crawling, pulling herself up the incline and struggling to stay ahead of the rising water. She looked so much like his Olivia that his heart leapt into his throat and he almost called out... but then the current spun him and he was pulled away from the big ship again.

He was thrown within reach of the lifeboat and hands were stretching out for him, yelling his name. Instinctively, he lifted up the boy first and the child was pulled from his grasp. He reached out to be lifted aboard himself, and just as someone's fingertips brushed his, the willful current snatched him back again, pushing the lifeboat away along the crest of a wave.

Ben swam hard towards the boat again, and at that moment a massive sound split the night... a thunderous tearing of iron and steel. Ben looked back towards the Titanic and saw that one of its enormous funnels had torn free. He watched as the towering steel cylinder loomed above him like a falling mountain.

Directly in its path, he knew he was about to die the instant before it happened. When he cried out, he was crying for Olivia, who he realized would be left all alone in the world when he was gone.

Chapter Thirty-Two

Above the din, Olivia heard an anguished cry cut short as the towering funnel hit the water. She was thankful that her eyes were still stinging and blurred because she knew that people had been crushed by its fall.

Everything would begin to unravel quickly now, she knew. Any semblance of order was gone.

The lifeboats were all pulling clear of the ship now that it was going down fast. (She knew they were afraid of being pulled under.) Her only hope was to just stay out of the cold water for as long as she could.

The Titanic had listed to such an angle that Olivia was sliding down the deck towards the sinking front of the ship and she had to grab onto a nearby railing. She could feel it moving now, and the back end rose up higher and higher in the darkness. It was a terrifying feeling… like the whole world was tilting out of control.

Things began to slide. Deck chairs flew like deadly cannonballs past Olivia, and people rocketed by her as they tumbled down the steep deck into the frothy currents. Something banged into her shoulder hard as it sped by... nearly knocking her loose. She covered her head and braced herself while struggling to maintain her grip.

There was a brittle crash that sounded like a thousand dishes breaking all at once. It seemed to go on forever as furniture throughout the ship slid free and tumbled over. The noise was deafening and the whole time the huge ship continued to tilt forward like some horrifying carnival ride.

Then, the floor near Olivia began to splinter. Throughout the hull, Olivia heard pops and cracks like fireworks had been set off in the belly of the ship... the sounds of bolts splitting along seams and steel ripping against steel. The floorboards on the deck erupted into a splintered line and the ship jolted so hard that it rattled her teeth.

A sound rose up into the night unlike any ever heard... and then the greatest ship built by man—fifty thousand tons of iron, wood, and steel— ripped in half beneath Olivia.

She managed to hold on to the railing as the back of the ship suddenly fell with stomach-lurching speed. When it hit the water, it kicked up a massive wave and jarred Olivia with such force that she was thrown up and over the side.

She fell almost fifty feet down to the icy water and by the time her life vest pulled her up to the surface again, she saw that the current had thrown her far out into the darkness. The searing pain from the icy water assaulted her body again and her hand went up instinctively to make sure the package was still safely wedged under her vest.

The back half of the ocean liner seemed to have righted itself in the darkness... and Olivia even heard someone in the water yell out "The Titanic is staying afloat! We're saved!" She knew better, though.

It was almost too dark to see, but Olivia could make out the shapes of people—hundreds of them—swarming over the decks along the back of the ship. Within a few moments, the ship began to tilt again… quickly this time. She could hear screams and cries for help and saw people jumping from the sides.

In the light reflected from the Carpathia, Olivia could see the enormous propellers of the ship rising up and glistening in the darkness. If there were others in the water around her, they had gone silent now as, like her, they watched the last moments of the doomed ocean liner in speechless horror.

The back half of the ship slipped under the water with a silent, terrifying speed. A frothy current was stirred up at its base as the black water swallowed what remained until every trace of the towering ship disappeared completely beneath the surface.

The darkness was filled immediately with screams as the icy water stabbed at the hundreds of floating survivors. Sickeningly, the sound reminded Olivia of the cheering crowd at a baseball game.

They were dying.

So many of them were dying.

She had hoped to save them. She had tried…

Her whole body was numb now and Olivia realized that she, too, was most likely dying. She closed her eyes and found that she wasn't afraid at all. Then, as the world around her began to seem faded and distant, she heard the splashing of oars and people shouting nearby. Strong hands grabbed her vest roughly and she was being pulled out of the water.

Vaguely, she felt a rough woolen blanket being wrapped around her, but she was far too numb to know for sure.

She had just enough wits about her to realize that maybe she was being saved. Perhaps she wouldn't die after all. As she drifted off, that thought brought a weak smile to her lips.

Olivia awoke to the familiar glow of the service light set into the ceiling of her hidden cubbyhole. She was wrapped in blankets and engulfed in the warm comfort of her overstuffed linen bed.

She awoke slowly, feeling like she was still bobbing in icy cold water. She could feel the familiar comforting thrum of the Carpathia's engines vibrating the floor and the sway of the waves as they cut through the water.

Her body felt sore and her head was throbbing, but the feeling of safety and warmth seemed to make all of that pain seem distant and unimportant.

Bubs was with her.

He was beside the bed and when her eyes fluttered open, he almost jumped up and hit his head on the low-hanging pipes above.

"Olivia! You're awake!"

"I'm awake." Olivia confirmed groggily. "What happened? How did I get here?"

"Jimmy the Porter was on the lifeboat that pulled you out of the water. He said that they all thought you were dead for sure."

Olivia grinned weakly. "Me too." she said.

"We're on our way back to New York with all of the survivors we picked up." Bubs said. "There's hardly even any room to stand up out there. They had you laying on one of the tables in the dining hall where they've setup an infirmary, but once we saw that you were going to be okay, I asked if we could move you down here so you would be more comfortable."

"Thank you, Bubs." Olivia smiled gratefully. "You were right. This is much more comfortable than those metal tables would have been."

Bubs grinned back at her proudly.

"How long has it been?" Olivia asked.

"It was yesterday morning when they brought you aboard. You've been asleep for a day and a half."

Olivia wasn't at all surprised by this. She felt like she had been sleeping a week.

"How many?" she asked, clearing her hoarse throat.

"How many what?" Bubs blinked.

"Survivors. How many did we save?"

Bubs shook his head. "They're still trying to count everybody, so nobody knows for sure. I heard my father telling the captain, though, that there were well over a thousand."

Olivia swallowed.

A thousand.

Originally, there had been only seven hundred. She had not saved everyone who would have perished, but she had saved some of them. Hundreds maybe. That counted for something.

"Olivia," Bubs began carefully. "I have to ask... why were you even out in the water? What were you trying to do?"

Suddenly remembering, Olivia reached up to her chest where she had tucked the small package into her life vest. "There was a package!" she said, trying to control the rising panic. "I had it in my..."

"It's here." Bubs said, reaching behind him and pulling the paper-wrapped parcel from the top of the steamer trunk. "You were clutching it against your chest so tightly that they had to pry it away... even while you were passed out."

Olivia took the package and was relieved to find it still intact. The scrawled address on the outside had been unrecognizably smeared, and the paper was brittle and water stained, but otherwise it looked fine.

"What is it?" Bubs asked curiously.

"I don't know." Olivia admitted, pushing it carefully under her pillow. Her head was pounding furiously now from the sudden movement and she had to lie down again and press her hand up over her eyes.

Bubs was about to ask more, but was interrupted by a light knock on the service door that led out to the corridor.

"It's probably my mom." Bubs whispered. "She's been stopping by to check on you just about every hour."

But when the door opened Olivia was horrified to see the blackened and misshapen face of Curly Reynolds bending down and peering in through the tangle of pipes at her.

He's come to kill me! was her first thought. *He thinks I cheated him in the sweepstakes and now he's here to beat me to within an inch of my life!*

Instead of an enraged glare, though, Curly was looking through the pipes at her with a solemn, almost humble expression.

"Olivia." he said softly. "I need to have a word with yeh."

No "*bilge rat*" this time. He had called her by her name.

It had to be a trick. He knew that he couldn't reach her through the tangle of pipes, so he was trying to lure her closer. She wouldn't fall for it.

Curly saw that she wasn't moving and he could guess why.

"Don't be afraid, little girl." he said in his rough voice that sounded so strange when he wasn't yelling over the noise of the engine room. "It's about your father. Somethin'… somethin' has happened."

It was a trick… she knew it had to be. Bringing her father into it was low… even for Curly. Still, though, she found herself sitting up in her bed and moving closer.

"Olivia, don't!" Bubs hissed, but there was something about the look in Curly's eyes that made a lump rise suddenly in her throat.

Curly cleared his throat. He looked uncomfortable. His brutish features were not accustomed to showing emotion. "Yer father, he… eh… went to help with the lifeboats. He brought back one group… saved a lot of lives. He went back out again and there was… er… an accident. He jumped out to save a kid, but then was swept away. My men tell me that he was a hero. They couldn't reach him before the funnel fell. There was no way for them to---"

216

But Olivia was shaking her head now, refusing to hear more.

It was impossible. Her father was alive! This was a trick! Curly was lying!

But then Curly was handing her something through the pipes and without understanding, she reached out and took it.

She saw that it was her father's things. Everything he owned wrapped up in a neatly tied bundle. On top was a picture: Olivia with her father and her mother. It was the picture her father kept beside his bunk. In the picture they were all smiling, the way they were when they were all together as a family before her mother's accident.

…and in that instant, Olivia knew that it was true.

Her father was gone.

Then, even worse was the crushing, unbearable realization that came next: *it was her fault.*

She had saved so many hundreds of lives but in exchange God had taken her father.

She had changed history… and the universe had broken after all.

Chapter Thirty-Three

Nothing mattered to Olivia anymore.

When her mother had died last year, her father had been there and together they had shared the pain and loss and helped each other get through the worst of it. This time, though, she had no one.

Bubs tried to help in his own way. He brought her meals regularly, only to come back hours later and find them still untouched. Although she could hear commotion throughout the ship—day and night—she never left her hidden room.

She lay unmoving for almost two days, curled up in her bed with the picture of her father and mother pressed up against her chest.

My fault. It's all my fault.

She was numb. Not her body—her muscles had long since regained their feeling. No, it was her mind that was submerged in the icy water now. It was her thoughts that hurt more than her body ever had.

On Thursday afternoon, three days after the morning the Titanic had slipped under, Olivia finally crawled out through the tangle of pipes and into the corridor outside her cubbyhole.

The top deck was packed with people huddled in blankets against the cold wind. Although there must have been hundreds of people lining the rails and sitting in chairs, nobody spoke. The only sound was the wind howling through the rigging above.

When Olivia looked around, she realized that everyone on the deck wore the same hollow expression. Like her, nearly everyone here had also lost someone they knew or loved. She could see the loss and pain of her own heart reflected in the eyes of every person she passed.

Nearby, a woman lay in a deck chair with a small, dark-skinned boy huddled against her chest. He was sleeping soundly despite the cold wind whipping around him. The woman stared off at nothing in particular. Her eyes were haunted and distant.

When Olivia turned, she was surprised to see the Statue of Liberty passing. *Were they back in New York? Had it been so long already?*

Although she wasn't high up in the crow's nest, Liberty's face still seemed to loom close by. Perhaps it was a trick of the afternoon shadows, but her weathered expression seemed just as sorrowful and stricken as the passengers that lined the deck watching her in solemn silence.

The city itself was lost in a grey haze, but Olivia could see other ships all around them, many lined with onlookers and some with photographers eagerly snapping pictures.

Olivia turned to go, and in that moment the little boy sleeping next to her raised his head and looked at her, narrowing his bright green eyes with a fiery intensity.

"Remember your task, Miss Grace." he whispered coldly, barely audible above the wind. "I want that package. Let's not forget the task at hand."

Olivia's chest tightened.

She blinked at him and stuttered. "What did you say?"

But the little boy had already laid his head back against his mother's chest and was sleeping soundly again.

Olivia shuddered, and her chill no longer had anything to do with the cold wind that wailed mournfully through the rigging above.

Olivia passed through the crowd warily now, looking at each exhausted face as a potential threat. Dumas could be anyone and anywhere. Olivia felt like a rabbit being hunted by a lion. Dumas would never stop until she got what she wanted.

Back in her tiny crawlspace, Olivia dug under her pillow and retrieved the wrapped brown parcel. She held the innocuous package as if it were a live snake in her hands, remembering Chuck's frantic message to her aboard the Titanic.

"You cannot let that package get in the hands of Dumas. If she gets hold of what's in that package, she'll be almost unstoppable."

Dumas was already able to reach back through time and harass her from over a century away. Olivia couldn't imagine a more terrible power than that... but Chuck had gone through a lot of trouble to warn her, so it must have been something truly frightening indeed.

I should go above decks and throw it over the railing right now. Olivia thought. *Then I could be done with Dumas altogether.*

But would that really stop her from getting it? Olivia thought it may not.

I'll burn it, then. She decided angrily. *Burn it and be done with Dumas and HistCorp and time travelling forever...*

Olivia paused, still clutching the package indecisively. After days of grief and fear and pressure, her thoughts were sluggish and frayed... but through this cloud, a glimmer of an idea crept into her mind.

The image of the Titanic's massive smokestack bearing down on her father flashed through her head and she closed her eyes to shut it out.

There are other timelines, Chuck had told her. Her father was dead here, but...

"I changed history once." She said aloud to her empty crawlspace. "I could do it again."

Self-conscious of her own voice in the silence, Olivia grew quiet once more and bit her lip thoughtfully. She remembered the HistCorp informational video and the millions of invisible wormholes flowing through the air around her. Any one or a dozen of them could be ears for Dumas. She imagined someone in a white coat, sitting at a terminal over a hundred years from now, watching and listening to her as she sat in her tiny room with the package clutched in her hands.

She had to imagine that they would *always* be listening. Chuck had told her once that the only way to avoid Dumas was to keep moving... never stay in one place too long.

Olivia looked again at the small cubby she had called home for all of these months, nestled in the tangle of pipes with the bright service light up above her linen-stuffed mattress. She had always felt so safe here... but she suddenly understood that had been because her father had been close by. Now, she realized, this place was no longer her home, and leaving it wouldn't be as hard as she would have once imagined. .

Even before the engines of the big steamship came to a complete stop, Olivia could hear the din from the crowd outside.

The sinking of the Titanic was the biggest news story of the century and every newspaper in the world was there fighting for a piece of it. Rostron had all hands on duty to prepare for what would undoubtedly be a chaotic scene at the pier.

Olivia moved quickly and gathered up everything that she needed. It broke her heart to leave the big old steamer trunk that had belonged to her mother, but she knew that she had to travel light if she had any hope of getting away. She tied up everything into a bed sheet and took a deep breath, looking around for one last time.

Before she turned to go, she hesitated and bit her lip, then decided to snatch up a scrap of paper and hastily scratch out a note with the stub of a pencil she had beside her bed.

Bubs,

I don't want you to worry about me. I can't explain why, but I've got to keep moving. This timeline has nothing left for me, but maybe I can use whatever is in this mysterious package to help me jump into another. Please don't worry about me. Thank you for believing in me and being my friend when I needed one most. I will always remember you for that.

Yours always,
Olivia

Olivia set the note on the steamer trunk and slipped quietly through the tangle of pipes for the last time.

On the upper deck, the survivors, crew, and Carpathia passengers stood together shoulder-to-shoulder facing the mob that was awaiting them on the pier. Some held hands, others held each other close. A strange kinship had grown amongst them all these past few days and they knew and understood that they had collectively shared an experience that no one else in the world would ever truly understand. Their faces were stony and grim as they stood there in the cold, side-by-side for one last time.

The gangplank was extended and as the first of the Titanic's survivors began to disembark, the flash of magnesium bulbs was like a fireworks display. Reporters that packed the pier all began yelling and calling out at once, clamoring for a story.

It took Olivia almost an hour to slip off the ship amid the chaos, but soon she was clear of the crowds and moving down the pier towards the city. It was a relief to see *her* New York and not the glass and steel alien world that it would later become. Despite this sense of homecoming, she also felt a twinge of fear at being on her own for the first time. In Evie's body, others had seen her as an adult and she had been able to fool them. Here, she was just a twelve-year-old girl with all of her belongings slung in a sheet over her back.

Olivia jumped when there was a light tap on her shoulder. She spun to see Bubs there with his big coat pulled up around him and his arms crossed expectantly. "Going somewhere?" he asked.

"Bubs, what are you doing here? You need to get back onboard before your parents miss you."

"They'll be fine." Bubs shrugged. "I left them a note." He looked at the bundle slung over Olivia's shoulder and motioned meaningfully at a similar bundle he held in his own arms. "So where are we going?"

"*We?*" Olivia balked. "What do you mean 'we'? There is no 'we'. I'm going this way and you're going back to the ship where you belong."

Bubs laughed. "And miss out on the adventure of my life? I don't think so."

"Bubs. You're just a kid. This is serious."

"You're just a kid, too." Bubs shot back.

"I'm twelve." Olivia pointed out, as if that would prove that she was indeed capable of taking care of herself.

"Did you bring any food?" Bubs asked.

Olivia hesitated, mentally kicking herself for forgetting such a basic necessity.

As if reading her mind, Bubs opened his bag to reveal an overflowing supply of bread, cheese, fruit, and even some soup cans.

Still, Olivia shook her head. "Bubs, you really can't..."

"What about money?" Bubs interrupted. "How are you going to live?"

"I've got seven dollars." Olivia shot back. It had been all the money her father had in the world, tucked in among his belongings.

Bubs reached into his pocket and pulled out a wad of bills that had to easily amount to almost fifty dollars. Olivia's eyes widened and she instinctively pushed his hand down out of sight so nobody else could see it. "Where on earth did you get that much money?" Olivia whispered urgently. "Did you..." she darted her eyes around to make sure nobody was nearby and lowered her voice even more. "Did you steal that?"

Bubs looked offended. "No! Geez, Olivia. These are tips from the last few days. I've been running errands for all of the rich Titanic folks onboard and they've been throwing cash at me right and left. There's something about almost dying that makes people a lot more generous, I guess."

Olivia looked at him sharply. "Well put it away before someone knocks you over the head and takes it. We're not on the Carpathia anymore."

Bubs stuffed the wad of cash back into his pocket and looked at her meaningfully. "Still, don't you see, Olivia? You need me. You can't survive out there alone. Whatever you're about to do, you will have a much better chance of doing it with my help."

Olivia rolled her eyes dubiously at this, but inside she had a nagging feeling that he may actually be right. She looked at Bubs, then back at the city behind her.

Gritting her teeth, she finally made up her mind. "Fine." She relented at last. "But there are a couple of rules. First… we have to keep moving. We can't stop in one place for too long." She grabbed the sleeve of Bubs' coat and pulled him into a brisk pace beside her, turning left down a side street and then cutting across a small grassy area between some trees.

Bubs ran to catch up. "What? Why?"

"Because they're always listening." Olivia said tersely. "We need to assume that they are always listening. Somewhere in the future, there are hundreds of people sitting in front of computers and looking for us."

Bubs looked over his shoulder, not knowing what a computer was but still very unsettled by the idea that unseen people could be listening to them at any given moment. "Alright." he muttered nervously. "Lead the way."

Chapter Thirty-four

On the evening of April 22, 1912, Olivia and Bubs were in a small rented room about a hundred miles outside of Philadelphia.

The room was hot and humid, owing mostly to the radiator by the window that had been turned up as high as it would go. Olivia had loosened the valve just enough to let a jet of steam escape out, whistling loudly like a boiling teapot. The noise would drown out their conversation from anyone who may be eavesdropping… from the next room or across time and space.

A newspaper from four days ago lay on the bedside table. The headline splashed across its cover read:

CARPATHIA STEAMS THROUGH THE NIGHT TO RESCUE 1604 FROM TITANIC DISASTER!

When Olivia had first read about the Titanic in the future, there had only been 704 survivors. Olivia's actions had been responsible for saving nine hundred more people.

"And each of those people will go on to live their lives and have families and change the world in their own way." Bubs said, as if trying to fully grasp the enormity of it. "It's like this ripple in a pond that's going to grow and change more and more as the years go by. The New York you saw in the future may be completely different by now."

Olivia stood by the steaming radiator, silently looking out the window. As if reading her mind, Bubs continued. "Those people are alive now because of you. If you try to undo what you've done... wouldn't that be the same as killing them yourself?"

Olivia shook her head. "I can save my father without undoing everything." she said.

"How?" Bubs asked.

Olivia tensed up. In her hands, she held the unopened package that she had retrieved from the Titanic. "I don't exactly know how just yet." she admitted.

"So you're going to make a deal with Dumas then? She helps you save him somehow in exchange for the package?"

Olivia cringed, remembering Chuck's desperate plea to keep the package out of Dumas' hands. To make a deal with Dumas would be to betray him after all he had done to save her. She knew, though, that she would do anything if it meant a chance to save her father.

She looked down at the package. "I think I should open it." Olivia decided at last.

Bubs looked surprised. "Really?"

"I need to understand why Dumas wants this so badly if I am going to make any kind of decision about it."

Olivia turned over the small wrapped parcel in her hands one more time, then made up her mind and pulled at the corner of the paper. The water-damaged wrapping fell apart easily and revealed a small leather-bound journal inside.

Hesitantly, she thumbed it open and saw that, remarkably, the inside seemed to have remained dry and undamaged.

On the first page was written in spidery Victorian lettering:

M.N.: 1534

Bubs was by her side in an instant, reading over her shoulder. "Who is M.N.?" he asked aloud. Then: "Fifteen thirty-four? Is that… do you think that's a date?"

Olivia bit her lip thoughtfully. "That would make this journal almost four hundred years old. What on earth could Dumas want with this?"

Olivia turned the page and found it filled from top to bottom with the same close-spaced, spidery script. It wasn't written in English, though. In fact, it didn't appear to be any language she had ever seen. Mixed among the letters were odd symbols that she didn't recognize at all.

Olivia thumbed ahead a little more then stopped. There, the author had drawn a sketch that filled two pages. Bubs and Olivia stared at it together for a long time in thunderstruck silence.

"That's impossible." Bubs breathed quietly.

"Nothing is impossible." Olivia replied absently. Still, though, she didn't understand how this *could* be possible.

The image on the pages of the old journal quite clearly showed a picture of the Titanic, sinking into the sea at an angle. The artist had sketched a scattering of lifeboats in the water around it and… nearby… the familiar silhouette of the Carpathia.

"This hadn't happened yet." Olivia said fearfully

"Right." Bubs agreed. "If this was four hundred years ago, how could the author have known the future?"

"Not just any future," Olivia persisted. "This is *our* future. This is the future we made. The Carpathia didn't make it in time originally. Even if they could somehow know about the Titanic, how could this person have known the Carpathia would be there?"

... or had this picture changed when she had changed history? Olivia wondered. *Was this once a picture of just the Titanic, sinking alone in the night? Had this sketch from 400 years ago been transformed when the future had been altered?* The thought made Olivia's head hurt, and she found herself reluctant to turn the page. Impatiently, Bubs reached over and turned it for her.

There were several more pages of writing, then more pictures. There was an airplane, a light bulb, a Nazi swastika, and dozens of other pictures and symbols that Olivia recognized from her visit to the future.

When Olivia explained what the pictures meant, Bubs shook his head. "Why would that HistCorp woman want this journal so badly? To her, these are all in the past. They're not going to show her anything she doesn't already know."

Olivia ran her fingers thoughtfully over the cryptic writing. "But a person in 1534 had no way of knowing these things. This person could somehow see into the future." she said quietly.

She remembered then something that Chuck had told her.

"HistCorp can't see the future." Olivia realized. "They can see the past and they can see the present, but with all of their technology and resources, they've never been able to clearly see the future, and that's driven Dumas crazy. To a woman who can see anything, anywhere... it's her one blind spot."

Bubs pointed to the yellowed page of the old journal. "Maybe those symbols are a code to unlock the secret. Maybe someone in 1534 discovered the secret to seeing into the future and this journal is the guidebook on how they did it." Bubs shuddered. "Could you imagine? If someone could actually see into the future, they would be..."

"Unstoppable." Olivia said with a chill.

She started to close the journal, knowing now that despite her hopes for a trade, this book could never fall into the hands of Dumas. She would have to think of another way to get back to her father. Someone like Dumas could never be allowed to have this kind of power.

The final picture seemed to be unfinished and had ominous reddish droplets staining the page. It was a picture of a strange mushroom-shaped cloud. As her thumb slid past it, she saw that the remaining pages were blank and unfinished. Then, on the very last page, more writing caught her attention. This handwriting was much different… clearly a woman's elegant handwriting. For some reason, the text here had been written upside-down on the page. When she flipped the book over, she was surprised to find that, unlike the rest of the book, this note was in English. Upon seeing the first word, Olivia suddenly found it hard to breathe.

Reading over her shoulder, Bubs actually gasped aloud above the hiss of the radiator.

> *Olivia,*
>
> *I am told that this journal may one day find its way into your hands. Although I cannot quite fathom such an improbable turn of events, I have experienced a great many things recently that have made me come to realize that nothing is quite as impossible as one imagines.*
>
> *This journal contains the key to our reunion. Guard it closely from those who would abuse it and guide it into the hands of those you trust.*
>
> *I love you so much, and… God willing… we will see each other again soon.*
>
> *Love,*
> *Mother*

Bubs swallowed hard as Olivia re-read the page a second, then a third time. "But you told me that you mother is dead." he sputtered.

"Nine hundred passengers on the Titanic were dead until I changed things." Olivia whispered, trying to wrap her head around it… suspecting a trick from Dumas but knowing in her heart that somehow this really was a message from her mother, written over 400 years in the past.

Bubs shook his head in disbelief. "But… this is impossible. You know that, don't you?"

Olivia ran her hand thoughtfully over the message from her mother. "Nothing is impossible." she whispered… and for the first time in days began to feel an ember of hope.

Bubs, perhaps feeling the weight of the moment, looked suddenly very pale. "That Dumas lady is not going to stop until she has this journal."

Olivia nodded slowly. " *'Guard it closely from those who would abuse it and guide it into the hands of those you trust. '*" she recited. "We've got to find a way to get this to Chuck."

"Over a hundred years in the future? How are we supposed to do that?" Bubs asked. "In case you hadn't noticed, we're just two kids here and we're all alone."

A splintery, scratching sound to Olivia's right caught their attention. Olivia's heart jumped when she saw that her hand, which she had been unable to move just days before, was now clutching a letter opener from the nearby desk and, with jerky, frantic motions, was carving letters into the wood surface there.

When her hand stopped moving, Bubs and Olivia stared down in silent wonder at the two words written there.

not alone

"Is that…" Bubs began slowly.

After all of the unexpected turns of fate that the past few days had brought her, Olivia met this newest revelation with a mixture of awe and relief. "Bubs," she said slowly. "I'd like you to meet Evie Deerbourne."

231

Author's Note:
About History

When I was a kid, I went with my family to see a movie called *The Final Countdown* about a modern-day United States aircraft carrier that gets sucked back in time to the days just before the Japanese attack on Pearl Harbor.

What an amazing idea! I was enthralled. These people had a chance to forever alter the course of human history and save thousands of lives... maybe even prevent a war...

The movie ended up teasing the audience, though, and they never got their chance to alter history. I was so frustrated and disappointed at the time... and I realized when I began writing this story that it was my chance to make up for that disappointment. From the beginning, I knew that Olivia was going to change things in the way that we all dream we could.

Although this tale is quite obviously fictional, the setting and true events surrounding the Titanic disaster are woven into the fiction. The RMS Carpathia, a passenger steamer from the Cunard shipping lines, did in fact leave New York Harbor on April 11, 1912 for her rendezvous with destiny.

Harold Cottam was the young Marconi wireless operator on the ship and, of course, Author Rostron was the captain whose calm and decisive actions are legendary to this day.

The timeline of the Titanic's collision and a number of other details are historically accurate. The message Cottam received from the Titanic and the words and response of Rostron in the story mirror his words and actions in real life. Other details like the mileage sweepstakes, daily life aboard the Carpathia, and the final moments of the Titanic, are all based in truth as well.

Even with these details, however, I'll note that I took great liberties in making up almost everything else. There are a number of fantastic books on the true history of these events, and I'll readily admit that the historical account of the Titanic disaster and the Carpathia's rescue is even more compelling than any fiction I could ever create on my own.

Here are a couple of recommended reads to get you started on the subject:

A Night to Remember by Walter Lord

OTHER SIDE OF THE NIGHT: The Carpathia, the Californian and the Night the Titanic was Lost by Daniel Allen Butler

Titanic: An Illustrated History by Donald Lynch, Robert D. Ballard, and Ken Marschall

The Story of the Titanic As Told by Its Survivors by Jack Winocour

About the Author

Joe Tompkins works as a school Instructional Technology Specialist in Rockdale County, Georgia, where he lives with with his wife, Lisa, and their two wonderful daughters, Victoria and Michelle. He has written several novels, including the *Sleeping Beauty Overslept* series, also published by Autumn Harbor Press.

Joe also writes educational software for students of all ages.

You can find out more at www.gepetosoftware.com.

www.ingramcontent.com/pod-product-compliance
Lightning Source LLC
Chambersburg PA
CBHW031319170626
46807CB00002B/485